ULTRABALL

DEATHSTRIKE

BOOKS BY JEFF CHEN

Ultraball: Lunar Blitz
Ultraball: Deathstrike

ULTRABALL

DEATHSTRIKE

JEFF CHEN

 KATHERINE TEGEN BOOKS

An Imprint of HarperCollins Publishers

Katherine Tegen Books is an imprint of HarperCollins Publishers.

Ultraball #2: Deathstrike
Text copyright © 2020 by Jeff Chen

Library of Congress Control Number: 2019950096
ISBN 978-0-06-280269-9

Typography by Joel Tippie
19 20 21 22 23   PC/LSCH   10 9 8 7 6 5 4 3 2 1
❖
First Edition

To Jake and Tess, and their bottomless appetites for books

ULTRABALL

DEATHSTRIKE

Cryptomare Molemen

QB	Wraith
RB1	Smuggler
RB2	Cutter
CB1	Big Bertha
CB2	Catacomb

Farajah Flamethrowers

QB	Supernova
RB1	Afterburner
RB2	Firestorm
CB1	Asbestos
CB2	Inferno

Kamar Explorers

QB	Shootout
RB1	Tombstone
RB2	Lasso
CB1	Gunner
CB2	Scout

North Pole Neutrons

QB	White Lightning
RB1	Meltdown
RB2	Fuel Rod
CB1	Radioactive
CB2	Ion Storm

Yangju Venom

QB	Serpent
RB1	Fang
RB2	Viper
CB1	Rattler
CB2	Toxin

Saladin Shock

QB	Transformer
RB1	High Voltage
RB2	Live Wire
CB1	Electrocution
CB2	Discharge

Tranquility Beatdown

QB	Destroyer
RB1	Uppercut
RB2	Hammer Fist
CB1	Chokehold
CB2	Takedown

Taiko Miners

QB	Strike
RB1	TNT
RB2	Rock
CB1	Pickaxe
CB2	Nugget

STRIKE'S SECRET

THE FIRST GAME of the 2353 Ultraball season hadn't gone to plan.

This was supposed to be the year that the Taiko Miners went all the way, to win their first Ultrabowl. But the worst team in the league had shocked the Miners right from kickoff. Throughout the entire first half, the Cryptomare Molemen had outplayed the Miners with a brilliant game plan.

The Miners had regrouped during halftime. They had fought their way back into the game. With only thirty seconds left, the score was tied at 70–70. The Miners were driving. Strike had the ball in his hands.

Just the way he liked it.

In the huddle, Strike stared into the clear helmet visors of his four teammates, ending with TNT. His rocketback 1's lips were pinched with determination. He nodded at Strike and asked, "Same play?"

"You know what they say," Strike replied. "Why mess with . . . the best?" He cocked his head at Rock. "Why mess with . . . less?"

"I think what you're looking for is 'Why mess with success?'" Rock said. "I'll show you after the game. Page sixty-seven of my notebook."

Strike thumped Rock's and then TNT's chest plates with metallic clonks. "Okay, everyone. Digger three, fly." The Miners had been killing the Cryptomare Molemen with this play during the second half. It was so hard to defend, TNT immediately diving into the underground maze—Cryptomare Stadium's signature field feature— and then outmaneuvering every defender before blasting out of whatever exit was unguarded.

"As soon as I shoot out of the maze, throw me a bullet," TNT said. "Hard as you can."

His jaw clenched; he was a man on a mission. The deal he had made two years ago—betraying the Miners in order to keep his mom safe—had caused him to become Taiko Colony's public enemy number one. Now that his mom was safely hidden deep inside Taiko, TNT was a one-man wrecking crew.

Strike lined up over the solid steel Ultraball. His two

crackbacks stood on either side of him, ready to smash any defender racing in. *This is our drive. This is our game.* Strike checked the power bar on his heads-up display—at 5.6 percent, plenty of juice left for one killer play—then barked out the snap count through their helmet comm. "Hut one. Hut two . . ."

He trailed off in confusion as the Molemen shifted into a formation he didn't recognize. Two of them came rushing up front, and a third jumped atop their shoulders. The final two Molemen had set up far back but were now sprinting in at full speed.

What the frak are they doing? Strike thought. But he quickly shook his head back into the game. It didn't matter what the Molemen were doing. Strike would connect with TNT and finish them off. "Hut hut!" Strike yelled.

But even before he started to backpedal, the two remaining Molemen were already running at top speed toward their tower of teammates. The Molemen defender on the top of the tower grabbed both streaking teammates, one with the left arm and one with the right. The Molemen had formed a megarobot, the five players making up the giant's arms, body, and legs.

Strike stumbled, his legs frozen in place for a moment at the monstrous sight. He threw himself to the left as the Molemen's megabot flung one of its arms at him, whipping in the defender. It was all he could do to duck the incoming missile, the defender nearly locking a magnetic glove onto his shoulder plate.

But the other defender shot in a split second later, smashing a fist into Strike's helmet. His head whipped backward, his helmet flashing a blinding array of warning lights at him. The defender chopped at the Ultraball. Then a sharp kick blasted into his wrist. Even though Strike's glove electromagnets were engaged at full power, the ball popped out.

A barrage of voices jolted his eardrums, his teammates yelling, "Fumble!" over the helmet comm. Strike scrambled for the ball bouncing along the ground, but another defender pancaked him to the turf. By the time he had wrestled his way out, Molemen in smoky gray Ultrabot suits swarmed around the ball, punching and kicking at the Miners wearing bright blue.

"Copernicus hot!" called a voice.

Strike's heart leapt. TNT had somehow muscled out of the bottom of the pile, the Ultraball cradled in his arm. With a roar, he burst free, high-stepping and juking to shake off defenders. He scrambled toward the sideline, but two Molemen had him contained. There was no way he'd turn the corner toward the end zone.

"Go down, go down!" Rock screamed.

That was the safe choice, running out the clock and sending the game into overtime. But with two coded words, TNT told Strike everything he needed to know.

Reversing course and streaking toward the opposite sideline, Strike vaulted over one of the entrances to the underground maze and picked up speed. He looked over his shoulder just as TNT torqued his body in a crazy twist, heaving the Ultraball in a cross-field lateral. Its reflective steel surface gleamed in the overhead lights. The pass arced high, soaring across the field.

A Molemen defender gave chase. Strike kicked off the turf, leaping for the incoming ball. The defender jumped almost at the same time, the two players elbowing for position. Activating his glove electromagnets, Strike strained desperately to stretch his fingertips past the defender's.

But he couldn't do it. At the last moment, the ball snapped into the defender's grip.

Strike swung wildly at the Moleman, trying to knock the ball out as they fell. When they slammed back to the turf, Strike lashed out with a barrage of furious punches. One connected, smashing into the Ultraball. The Moleman bobbled it, and Strike slapped it away.

As Strike lunged for the loose ball, two other players crunched into him, everyone punching and kicking each other in a mad scramble. Just as Strike picked up the Ultraball, a defender popped out of the underground maze from below Strike and yanked it out of his grip before disappearing back into the maze.

More players crashed into Strike, collapsing him to the ground. He tripped and plummeted halfway into a maze entrance, trapped on its edge by the mass of players crushing him. He fought desperately to escape his coffin. Panic choked his throat as he struggled against the thousands of kilograms pinning him into place. He thrashed in a frantic attempt to break free, hyperventilating against the walls closing in around him. With a surge of terror-driven strength, he scrabbled out of the maze hole, taking deep, ragged breaths, trying to hold back his desperate need to click out of his Ultrabot suit. All he could do was watch as the Moleman who had stolen the ball from him popped out of the underground maze, broke a tackle, and took off in a run. With jukes and spins, the player faked out Pickaxe before hurdling clear over him.

TNT was the Miners' last hope, running three steps behind the Moleman in a race to the end zone. TNT kicked into fifth gear, somehow closing the gap. With a final leap, he launched himself upward, locking a magnetized glove onto the ball carrier's ankle. But with writhing twists, the Moleman dragged TNT along. TNT heaved backward, finally tripping up the Moleman. Off-balance, the Moleman spun around and lunged for the end zone.

The scoreboard flashed the final result:

Molemen   **77**

Miners   70

Strike dropped his head to the turf, still unable to move. His eyes fuzzed over as he tried to figure out what had happened.

The Molemen all raced into the end zone to celebrate their incredible win. The five of them leapt at each other in a frenzy of chest-bumping, ecstatic hugs, and turbo butt-slapping.

Strike slowly got to his feet, dragging his legs as he made his way to his teammates. The Miners had been out-strategized and outplayed by the Molemen, a win stolen from under their noses. This should have been an easy romp against the perennial cellar dwellers of the league. Instead, the Miners had started the season with a gut-punching loss, their backs already to the wall.

A sickening thought ate at him:

Had his horrible secret contributed to the loss?

TNT was on his hands and knees, slamming his fist into the turf. Strike went to give him a hand up, but TNT kept on going. "No," he moaned over the team's helmet comm. "No." He punched the ground harder and harder, divots flying.

"We'll come back from this," Strike said. "We've lost games before and come back stronger." As the Miners' coach, he had to say something. But his words came out empty, laced with disappointment.

"Going undefeated on our way to an Ultrabowl championship was my way of making everything right," TNT said, his voice hollow. He stopped punching and let his helmeted forehead thunk to the turf. "To you guys. To our fans." He turned toward Strike, his eyes bloodshot. "I have to work even harder. We all do. We have to go practice. Now."

It hadn't seemed possible to feel any worse than before, but now Strike's throat went dry. The Ultrabot suit felt tighter than ever, its armored panels seeming to squeeze his body like a hydraulic vise.

Pickaxe walked by, grumbling. "Not this again," he said with a scowl. "We need to rest and regroup. You sound just like Boom, with all her stupid frakkin' talk about nonstop practice."

The other Miners went quiet at the mention of last year's star rocketback, who had nearly died in the plan she had orchestrated to save Taiko Colony.

Rock stormed up to Pickaxe, bumping him chest to chest. "Don't you ever insult Boom again," he said. "Take that back. Right now."

Strike ran in between Pickaxe and Rock, pushing them apart. "Cut it out. Time to go shake the Molemen's hands." He motioned to the Ultraball players in dark gray, still celebrating.

Strike unclicked his helmet, the giant impactanium dome lifting up over his head and rotating back. The rest of the Miners followed his lead, approaching the Molemen.

One of the Molemen noticed the Miners approaching and went to meet Strike. With a pop and a hydraulic hiss, the Ultrabot suit's smoky gray helmet opened up and rotated back, the rookie quarterback's sweaty black hair covering half her face. She motioned for all her teammates to undo their helmets, too, the five Dark Sider girls heading toward the Miners.

There were so many questions Strike wanted to ask. In the ten-year history of Ultraball, no team had ever featured an entirely new roster, much less five Dark Siders. To keep it quiet all the way through the preseason was an unparalleled stroke of genius.

But before he could speak, Wraith leaned in close, the Molemen's quarterback whispering into Strike's ear. "Pretend like we're talking Ultraball." She clasped a gloved hand behind his neck, holding him in place. "Stay quiet and listen."

Strike's first instinct was to jerk away, but there was something in Wraith's voice. He gave her a tiny nod.

"I can't tell you details now," Wraith said. "We're being watched. But the rebellion needs you. Boom needs you."

Strike's eyes widened. "She's alive?"

"Shh." Wraith held him even closer. "She's safely hidden away, trying to gather an army to take down Zuna. Most Dark Siders don't want anything to do with this side of the moon, though. So she needs you. You're the key to it all."

"Me? I'm just a quarterback."

"You're way more than that." Wraith stole a glance over her shoulder toward a team of *LunarSports* reporters making their way over. "More later. Smile for the cameras." She pushed away. Waving toward fans in the stands, she walked off, the rest of the Molemen following her.

Strike stood frozen for a long moment before joining his teammates, Wraith's words ringing in his head.

RESULTS, WEEK 1

Molemen	**77**
Miners	70
Explorers	**63**
Venom	28
Neutrons	**105**
Beatdown	84
Flamethrowers	**84**
Shock	63

STANDINGS, WEEK 1

	Wins	Losses	Total Points
Neutrons	1	0	105
Molemen	1	0	77
Flamethrowers	1	0	84
Explorers	1	0	63
Beatdown	0	1	84
Miners	0	1	70
Shock	0	1	63
Venom	0	1	28

THE NEW-LOOK NEUTRONS

THE FIVE MINERS trudged toward the Ultraball tram, their armored boots clomping along the ground. The fans cleared the way, giving the players a wide berth. Strike led his team into the high-end tram, fitted out to the max by the Underground Ultraball League. Everyone silently docked their suits into their spots along the far wall before clicking out of them. Strike breathed a sigh of relief as his helmet rotated clear. His chest plate unclicked, and he jumped out of his suit as soon as the final panel opened.

The Fireball Five, nicknamed after the Fireball Blast tragedy that had taken the lives of at least one of each of their parents nine years ago, had never started with an opening-day loss. Guilt ate away at Strike. *How much longer can I hide my secret?*

And Wraith's words . . . Strike shook his head. It was incredible to hear that Boom was still alive, hidden on the Dark Side of the moon. But whatever her rebellion was, and as important as it was to stop Raiden Zuna, it would have to wait. This season was probably Strike's last shot to secure his teammates' futures. He had to redouble his efforts toward a singular goal: winning the Ultrabowl. Who did Boom think he was, anyway? Strike Sazaki was an Ultraball player, not the leader of a revolutionary army.

"Hey." TNT pointed to the TV hanging on the side of the tram, tuned to *LunarSports Reports*. "What the frak is going on?"

Strike turned to watch highlights of the Neutrons game. He blinked. "That can't be right."

"Who's that at quarterback?" Nugget asked.

"It's Fusion, dummy," Pickaxe said. "Who else would quarterback the North Pole Neutrons . . ." He trailed off, his mouth hanging open. "That's not Fusion."

Strike peered in, all of them crowding the screen.

The screen cut to a press conference, the five Neutrons sitting behind a table, all lined up on either side of the team's owner, Raiden Zuna.

A seething rage surged inside Strike. Zuna had fired his deadly Meltdown Gun at Boom during last year's

Ultrabowl in an attempt to kill her. But nothing had happened to him afterward. Minimal questioning. No arrest. Nothing.

"What happened to Fusion?" a reporter asked Zuna. "Why did you replace him with White Lightning, of all people? And what happened to Chain Reaction?"

Zuna stared silently at the reporter, his fiery glare burning a hole into the guy's head.

Strike squinted, studying the kids who were flanking Zuna. Chain Reaction was not among them. The brash superstar rocketback had been the North Pole Neutrons' focal point, their entire offense built around his playmaking abilities. The four-time league MVP held most of the Underground Ultraball League records and was the driving force behind the Neutrons' four straight Ultrabowl titles. White Lightning replacing Fusion at quarterback was surprising, but the Neutrons parting ways with Chain Reaction was astonishing.

Zuna's eyes narrowed, his focus on the reporter intensifying. "I'm going to go over this only one more time," he said. "Fusion and Chain Reaction played great for four years. They helped bring Neutron Nation four Ultrabowl titles. But as owner and general manager of the Neutrons, it's my responsibility to field the best team possible. Meltdown is my rocketback 1 now. White Lightning is my quarterback. The Saladin Shock made a major mistake in cutting him after last season. I capitalized on it.

White Lightning led us to a huge win today." He pointed to a stoic boy with black hair parted down the middle, his eyes sunken, dark folds of skin drooping under them.

"But how did you keep the quarterback and rocket-back 1 switches secret until just before kickoff?" another reporter asked. "You must have paid a fortune to pull this off."

A thin smile appeared on Zuna's face, the freeze thawing. "Can you get a load of this guy? Asking if Raiden Zuna has a lot of money is like asking . . . it's like asking if the guy who asked that question is a moron."

Nervous laughter rippled through the room. A camera focused on the reporter who'd asked the question, the guy's face going bright red. He tried to laugh along with his fellow reporters, but his bald head beaded up with flop sweat. "Sorry," he finally said. "Dumb question."

"But Mr. Zuna," a reporter from the *Lunar Times* asked, "didn't you lose a ton of money on last year's Ultrabowl? You bet heavily against there being a blackout in Neutron Stadium, and there was one. It's rumored that you lost most of your fortune on that bet alone. And then you spent forty million Universal dollars to buy *LunarSports Reports*. Your war chest has to be low at this point."

The crowd of reporters fell silent, an icy chill hanging over the room. Zuna gripped the edge of the table, his knuckles white. "Media people make up whatever they need to in order to support their liberal agenda," he hissed through clenched teeth. "Lies. That's why I bought *LunarSports Reports*, the only trustworthy media outlet. As of now, I'm revoking reporters' press passes if they're proven to be liars. So get out. And if I ever see you again . . ." He smoothed out his red jumpsuit before shooting glances at the Blackguards in the corners of the room. "Leave."

A low buzz went up in the audience. The *Lunar Times* reporter shriveled into his brown jumpsuit. Everyone else stared off in other directions, as if the guy didn't exist. Finally, the reporter slowly got to his feet and left.

Zuna stared down the rest of the room. "Now. Any other questions?"

After a pause, a person in the back of the room, dressed in the blue jumpsuit of Taiko Colony, stood up in a show of defiance. "You can't do that. Since when is the press censored?"

"My press conference, my rules," Zuna said. He motioned to the Blackguards, who quickly zeroed in on the man and lifted him off his feet.

"Hey!" the man cried. "Get your hands off me."

"Your press pass is revoked, too," Zuna said.

The man struggled, protesting as the Blackguards hustled him out and carried him away.

"Now," Zuna said, "are there any other questions? Smart questions?"

A *LunarSports* reporter got to his feet, glancing down to read off a cue card. "Mr. Zuna. Can you comment on the five Dark Siders now making up the Molemen's roster? Do the Dark Siders pose a threat to our safety?"

"I'm glad you asked," Zuna said. "Yes. What happened during last year's Ultrabowl was an act of terrorism. The Dark Siders are extremely dangerous. They're criminals. Felons. My people will be watching Wraith's and her teammates' every move. I will not allow terrorists to go unpunished." He raised a fist, squeezing it tight. "The Council of Governors isn't willing to do anything about it. But I am. I promise you that I will keep the moon safe. I will make the moon strong once again."

"But the Molemen are just Ultraball players," a guy in a beige jumpsuit said. "Really good ones, too, considering how they upset the Miners today. You can't really think all Dark Siders are terrorists . . ." He trailed off as Zuna motioned toward the Blackguards in the corners of the room. "Uh. Never mind."

"Since there are no more questions, I'll end by saying that Neutron Nation will take home our fifth straight Ultrabowl title," Zuna said. "We are that good. White Lightning will lead us to the promised land. That's a guarantee. End of press conference."

The screen cut back to replays of the Neutrons' game, White Lightning throwing a pass through a slingshot zone, the ball accelerating to a silver blur before slamming into Meltdown, cannonballing him across the goal line for a score.

Inside the tram car, the Miners all looked at each other in silence. Finally, Pickaxe said, "What the frak is going on? Last time I checked, White Lightning was the butt of the league. Cut by the Shock, in disgrace. Now he's the Neutrons' quarterback?"

"White Lightning is a joke," Nugget said. "Zuna must be losing his mind."

Rock's face was tense with concentration. "Zuna always has reasons for doing what he does. There must be something we're missing."

Someone knocked at the tram door, waving through the window, holding up a souvenir. "Time to go sign some more autographs," Pickaxe said. He grinned at TNT, giving him a friendly elbow to the ribs. "The fans all want a piece of me, the real star of the Taiko Miners."

Strike was glad for Pickaxe's attempt to break the ice, to get the old TNT's brash, funny side to show through. But TNT just nodded and pressed the button to open the tram door.

Pickaxe shot a look at Strike and shrugged.

The game had been over for two hours now, and despite the Miners losing, there was still a big crowd waiting for them. People at the front held out small rocks shaped like footballs, most of them elbowing their way to Strike, but many with their eye on TNT.

Strike took a deep breath. Bringing home a championship would finally give Taiko Colony something to be proud of. But for the five Miners, it was life and death. A win would secure all their futures, with unlimited opportunities laid at their feet.

If they failed . . .

He jolted as a kid popped up by his side. "Uh. Hi. Do you remember me?" It was a scrawny girl, her arms and legs sticks.

"Kind of," Strike said, his brow furrowing. "Where do I know you from?"

Rock pulled out his notebook, flipping through it. "Jasmine Tariq," he said. "Torch's little sister. After she got sick with dust poisoning last year, Torch sold some of our plays to Zuna in order to— Oof!" He held a hand over his ribs, where Strike had elbowed him.

Strike and Jasmine looked at each other uneasily. Finally, she cleared her throat. "About what Torch did . . ."

"It's okay," Strike said. "He did it for a good reason."

"No," Jasmine said. "I can't live with the guilt. I have to make it up to you. I'll be your personal assistant. I'll follow you around, do anything you need. I'll clean waste recyclers. Dig field pits. Anything."

"Really, it's okay," Strike said. "Those plays didn't even affect anything last year."

"Give me a chance," Jasmine said, her hands clasped

together. "Ask me to do something. Anything."

Strike looked over to Rock. "You need anything?"

"Can you gather information about the Dark Siders on the Molemen's roster?" Rock asked. "Not just their Ultraball skills and tactics, but if they might have ulterior motives, as Zuna claims."

Jasmine faltered for a long moment, but then she nodded. "I'm on it. I collected and analyzed statistics for the Flamethrowers back in the day. I was good at it, too. I'll find out everything there is to know. You'll see, Strike. I'm going to be the best personal assistant you ever had."

She made to run off, but Rock kept going. "I'd also like to know more about why the Neutrons replaced Fusion and Chain Reaction."

Jasmine paused. "Okay. I'll see what I can—"

"Speaking of the Neutrons, can you analyze their gameplay, identifying the weaknesses in their new defensive schemes?"

"Seriously?" Jasmine said. "I'll try, but—"

"Give it a rest," Strike said. "You can't really expect her to analyze the Neutrons' game."

"She's Torch's sister," Rock said. "I would bet twenty hardtack bars that she knows a great deal about Ultraball." He paged through his notebook. "That reminds me. I've always wanted to know more about how hardtack bars are produced, and why no one can make them taste good. Can you take a tram to New Beijing Colony and— Oof!"

He held his side, where Strike had elbowed him again.

"You better get going before he asks you for anything else," Strike said to Jasmine.

"You won't regret this," Jasmine said. "I'll find out everything there is to know. About everything." She raced away, zigzagging between fans, threading through the smallest of spaces.

"Think she'll actually find out anything useful?" Strike asked.

"I'd bet everything that she does," TNT said. "Making up for the past . . ." He bit his lip. "We'll both make up for our pasts." He motioned to the Ultraball tram. "Eight weeks left until the Ultrabowl. And just one week to prepare for our biggest game of the regular season. Come on. Enough with the autographs. Let's go practice."

Strike nodded. In seven days, they'd have to face their rival Neutrons—at Neutron Stadium. He rubbed his left shoulder, wincing as phantom pains shot down the length of his arm.

MINERS TROUNCED IN EMBARRASSING UPSET

By Aziz Chang, Executive Reporter

The Miners were demolished by the league's perennial cellar dwellers, the Molemen, in what should have been an easy win. Strike failed, allowing himself to be surprised by the Molemen's completely new roster of Dark Siders. Many have questioned whether Strike is still the right person to be the Miners' general manager. After still not clearing his name in connection with several crimes—including throwing last year's Ultrabowl in a crooked betting scheme—he would be wise to take appropriate actions.

Meanwhile, the North Pole Neutrons dominated the Tranquility Beatdown, annihilating them, 105–84. The Neutrons, unfazed by the two changes in their roster, are poised to take their unprecedented fifth Ultrabowl title in a row. White Lightning is even better at quarterback than Fusion, able to do what the old quarterback could do and much more—a shrewd, bold move by the team's owner, Raiden Zuna. Additionally, the replacement of their former star rocketback, Chain Reaction, did not affect the

Neutrons whatsoever. Meltdown stepped into the rocketback 1 role like a true hero, earning early consideration for league MVP. Raiden Zuna has the early edge for the General Manager of the Year award.

White Lightning and Meltdown are the new faces of the North Pole Neutrons, and the future of Neutron Nation looks stellar. Already with a commanding lead in the season tiebreaker of total points scored, the Neutrons continue to reign unparalleled as the top dogs of the Underground Ultraball League. Raiden Zuna has done something no other team owner has ever done: guided his team to a grand dynasty that may very well last forever.

In an exclusive interview with *LunarSports Reports*, Mr. Zuna commented on the win, the Neutrons' outlook for the season, and more. "The North Pole Neutrons have never looked better," he said. "This five-man roster outshines last year's by a wide margin. No other team in the league stands a chance. The smart money—including mine—is on my Neutrons to win it all."

When asked about the Molemen and their new roster, Mr. Zuna said, "It's unbelievable that the Underground Ultraball League is doing nothing, not even investigating them, considering the destructive act of terrorism taken by the last Dark Sider to play Ultraball. So it's up to me. I will be investigating every one of them, especially their quarterback, Wraith. And I doubt that yesterday's theft of nuclear reactor components from North Pole Colony was a coincidence. I will exact vengeance on anyone who dares to threaten the safety of the United Moon Colonies."

Rallies supporting Mr. Zuna's calls for counterterrorism have taken place across the moon, in almost all twenty-one United Moon Colonies. According to the latest polls, 81 percent of citizens are calling Mr. Zuna a national hero for taking it upon himself to do what the Council of Governors will not.

THE EARTHFALL EIGHT

It HAD BEEN months since Strike had been in Governor Katana's office. The last time had not gone well. Right after the Ultrabowl, the governor of Taiko Colony had ordered Strike to appear, to explain why the Miners had been disqualified in Ultrabowl X. It had taken hours of stammering and bumbling through explanations for Strike to appease the governor. Even then, Katana hadn't seemed convinced that the Miners were fully on the up-and-up.

Now, Strike and Rock sat inside Governor Katana's office, waiting for the most important person in Taiko Colony to speak. He had been staring at a handheld holo-screen for almost a minute since they had been shown into the room, and he still hadn't said a word. Strike was captivated by the piece of high tech in the governor's hands. After Earthfall, almost everyone in Taiko Colony had had to hock all their belongings, including their government-issued phones, just to pay for food and housing. The images dancing above the holoscreen were magical.

Just as Strike was about to clear his throat and break the uncomfortable silence, Governor Katana tossed the device onto his desk. He pushed it forward. "What do you make of this?" he asked.

Strike read the headline before exchanging a nervous glance with Rock. "*LunarSports Reports* makes up all sorts of crazy stuff."

"Problem is that people believe it." The governor leaned back in his chair. "Even though the numbers they quoted are false—the *Lunar Times*'s poll had Zuna's approval rating at sixty-one percent, not eighty-one percent—there is no doubt that he is gathering support." He made air quotes and spoke in a mocking tone. "'The only person brave enough to fight terrorism.'"

"Boom wasn't a terrorist," Strike said. "She saved Taiko Colony."

Katana shrugged. "One thing I learned early in my career: the truth is what people believe it is." He sat forward, interlacing his fingers in front of him. "What do you make of Wraith?"

"She's a great quarterback. And strategist." He let out

a long breath. "She surprised us yesterday."

"That's not what I meant." Katana pursed his lips, considering his words. "Zuna's accusations about her stealing nuclear weapon parts from North Pole Colony. Could they be true?"

"No," Strike said. "That's ridiculous."

"Is it?" Katana shifted, narrowing his eyes. "Those components went missing out of a high-security facility. One of Zuna's. Don't you find it coincidental that Boom triggered the blackout during last year's Ultrabowl with the help of components that she stole from Saladin Colony? History seems to be repeating itself."

Strike opened his mouth, but he had no idea how to deny the governor's statements. Wraith could easily be up to something, just like Boom had been.

The governor leaned back and collapsed into his chair, suddenly looking exhausted, wrinkles all over his age-spotted face. "Look, Strike. I appreciate that you saved Taiko Colony and our underground ice deposits from falling into Zuna's hands. I really do." He rubbed his eyes with the palms of his hands, taking a deep breath. "But Boom was trouble. Why couldn't you have just won the Ultrabowl on your own? I lost a ton of money betting on the Miners. So did a lot of people in Taiko."

Strike spoke through gritted teeth. "I wanted to win more than anything. I thought we had it all wrapped up when—"

The governor put up his hands. "Forget it. I shouldn't have brought up the past. It doesn't matter. What's important is the future. Zuna is more powerful than ever now. Calling out Boom and Wraith as terrorists was a stroke of genius. He's playing on people's fears, and they're eating up every word. Do you realize why he's pushing for the Council of Governors to hit the Dark Siders with a tactical military strike?"

"To get back at Boom, obviously," Strike said.

"Wrong," Katana said. "To gain power. To gain support. If he can get hold of fourteen votes, he'll be able to control the Council and do anything he wants. He's closer than ever now."

Rock's eyes widened. "That's not possible," he said. "He's a criminal. He should be in jail."

"You have to accept reality," Katana said. "That's why I called you into my office today." He stood up, coming around to the front of his desk and perching on it. Crossing his arms, he frowned. "The Council of Governors has been able to hold Zuna off, but it hasn't been easy. I need help. From you."

"Me?" Strike said. "What can I do?"

"What are the Dark Siders up to?" the governor asked. "Are they planning some sort of rebellion?"

Strike tensed before he could stop himself. He tilted his head, trying to look confused. "How would I know?"

"Don't treat me like an imbecile," Katana said. "You

don't have to tell me which Dark Siders you're talking to. I just need to know if we can trust them. My informants have told me that Zuna is up to something. Something huge. Considering what Boom was able to pull off during last year's Ultrabowl, the Dark Siders could be our greatest allies. But if they have their own hidden agenda, they could be our greatest threat."

"Wait," Strike said. "Back up. You think Zuna is up to something huge? Like what?"

"Not sure," the governor said. "All I know so far is that there's a lot of suspicious activity going on in and around North Pole Colony. I even got a bizarre report of a big footprint in the Tunnel Ring near North Pole station."

The hairs on the back of Strike's neck rose. "Was it a wraith's footprint?" he asked. The old folktales about something haunting the Tunnel Ring after dark were just stupid ghost stories to frighten kids. Weren't they?

"Don't be ridiculous. It was probably just one of my agents seeing things in the dark. It's easy to get spooked inside the Tunnel Ring at night." Katana leaned in, lowering his voice. "But there's no doubt that something moon-shattering is going down. I've even wondered if Zuna is allowing those nuclear parts to be stolen and taking a cut of the profits. Or secretly using them to build his own private nuclear arsenal."

"Not even he would do that," Rock said. "Would he?"

"I wouldn't put anything past him. He's hell-bent on

gaining control of the Council of Governors, and the best ways to do that are through money and intimidation." He looked to a giant picture of the Miners mounted on the wall, signed by each member of the Fireball Five. "How do you like your chances this year?"

Strike's eyebrows pinched together as he considered the sudden change in topic. "We'll try our best. We always do."

Katana interlaced his fingers, squeezing hard. "I wasn't sure if I should tell you this. The last thing you need is extra pressure. But you're more an adult than a child. Frak, you're the general manager of an entire Ultraball franchise. You deserve to have all the facts." He took a deep breath, cracking his knuckles. "My sources tell me that Zuna is doubling down. He's bet his entire remaining fortune on his Neutrons winning this year's Ultrabowl. If he succeeds, he won't need the Council of Governors to launch a military strike. He'll be able to make it happen all on his own."

Katana paused, letting the stunned silence hang over the room. "You're both too young to remember Earth-fall. An entire planet—over thirty billion people—dead, within the course of a single day. All because of eight bloodthirsty dictators, fighting each other for control of the Earth. I'm not exaggerating when I say that Zuna is cut from the same cloth as those eight tyrants."

Strike and Rock exchanged a wide-eyed glance. They'd

heard lots of stories about the Earthfall Eight, but more as monsters out of legends than as real people.

"I don't know what Zuna is planning, but I'd bet it's even bigger than his scheme to take over and destroy Taiko Colony last year," Katana said. "We have to stop him. Cutting off his finances is the best way to do that. If you guys keep his Neutrons from winning the Ultrabowl, he'll lose all his money. All his power."

The claustrophobia mounted in Strike's chest, a feeling like all the walls were closing in on him. He looked at the four Ultrabowl plaques mounted in the governor's office—every one of them a runner-up award. As if Strike didn't need a title badly enough. Now it was up to him to stop Raiden Zuna, a man the governor had just put in the same league as the Earthfall Eight?

Strike squeezed his fists tight. It was unfair for the governor to put the fate of the entire moon upon his shoulders. "We'll be up on the victory stand this year," he said.

But not for Katana. Not for anyone else but Rock, TNT, Pickaxe, and Nugget.

SHOWDOWN VS. THE NORTH POLE NEUTRONS

GAME DAY.

Every time the Miners battled the Neutrons, it was an explosive game of smashmouth, ground-pounding Ultraball. It was impossible to ever be confident against a team like the Neutrons, but Strike was feeling good. He'd come up with a perfect way to cover up his secret for one more week. A passing game focusing on short throws—ones he could easily complete—would make for a killer surprise strategy against the Neutrons. It had taken a while for everyone to get on board with it, but Strike had the team convinced that it was going to pay off. Even he was starting to believe it.

On their way to North Pole Colony, the Miners sat

together inside an Ultraball tram zooming through the Tunnel Ring, listening to Rock go over the game plan. Jasmine sat next to Rock as his makeshift assistant, feeding him papers filled with detailed gameplay notes. "We'll have to be careful of the Neutrons' Nuclear Fallout defensive scheme," he said. "It's a big improvement on their Nuclear Waste defense." He swayed as the tram jolted and slowed as they came to their next stop. "The Neutrons will drop Meltdown into Ion Storm's crackback slot whenever we look to be setting up any formation similar to a . . . to a . . ." He trailed off, looking out the window.

"To a slingshot V," Jasmine said, completing Rock's sentence. "Right?"

Strike nodded. He'd been skeptical of having Jasmine work for them as a gofer, but she'd proven quick on the uptake. *Maybe it won't be so bad having her around*, he thought.

The tram halted, making its automated stop at Moon Dock station. Rock focused even harder on something in the distance, his neck craned forward. "That's odd. Very odd."

"What's odd?" Strike asked.

"Besides Rock, you mean?" Pickaxe said. He laughed, but no one joined him. "What? It was funny." He pointed to Rock's notebook. "Aren't you going to write that down in your list of jokes?"

"Uh-huh," Rock said, his attention unwavering from whatever it was he was studying. Leaning into the side of the tram, he got so close his nose smooshed against the glass window. The door slid open and he poked his head out.

"I'll write it down for him," Jasmine said. "Should that go under 'Witty Humor' or 'Self-Deprecating One-Liners'?"

"Never mind that." Strike peered over Rock's shoulder. "What are you looking at?"

"The airlock door," Rock said.

"What about it?" Strike focused on the massive impactanium door in the distance, involuntarily shuddering at the endless expanse of black death on the other side of it. This empty station had been rendered useless after Earthfall, since no one had any reason to use the lone airlock separating the United Moon Colonies from outer space. But the Council of Governors had mandated that all trams stopped here, to remind people of the horrors the Earthfall Eight had unleashed upon humanity.

"Why isn't it dusty?" Rock asked, his brow furrowed in concentration. "This station doesn't have daily maintenance. The Cryptomare engineers have their hands full keeping the other stations running."

"How could you possibly notice dust on a door?" Jasmine asked.

"He notices everything," Nugget said. "He noticed

when Pickaxe didn't poop for four straight days last month."

Pickaxe flushed red. "I'll poop on *you*," he muttered.

Nugget snickered. "Except that you couldn't, you were so stopped up!"

Rock pulled out his notebook. "I'll be right back."

"What are you doing?" Strike asked, catching the back of Rock's jumpsuit. "We have a lot more game planning to go over."

"Aw, let him do it," Nugget said. "Five hardtack bars says he makes it there and back before the doors close."

"I'll take that bet," Pickaxe said. "Easiest five hardtack bars ever."

"Everyone, focus on the North Pole Neutrons," Strike said. "Rock is not going to run—"

"I'll do it!" Jasmine said. She sprinted out the doors, taking off like a shot.

"She'll never make it . . ." Pickaxe trailed off as the girl accelerated, her legs blurs of motion. "You know what? She might actually make it."

Jasmine put on a crazy burst of speed, jumping over benches, hurtling around lampposts. She stopped momentarily to look at the huge airlock door, and then sprinted back toward the tram.

A series of beeps sounded, signifying that the tram was preparing to leave the station. Strike nudged Rock. "Bet you ten hardtack bars that she doesn't make it."

Rock studied the little girl zipping back. He made a quick calculation in his notebook. "Let's make it twenty."

Strike peered nervously at all the numbers in the notebook. "How about we keep it at ten? Or maybe let's just call it off."

"Too late. I agree to the original bet," Rock said.

"She's huffing and puffing," Strike said. "Bet you didn't factor fatigue into your calculations."

"Ha," Pickaxe said, jabbing his brother with an elbow.

"Actually, I did," Rock said. "She's not slowing down as much as I thought she would." He beamed at Strike and Pickaxe, pointing as Jasmine deftly hurdled a set of benches.

"Ha!" Nugget said. He stood up, wiggling his butt at his brother.

Pickaxe quickly punched it, making Nugget shriek.

The final beeps sounded, and the tram doors started to close. With a final burst, Jasmine sped through just before the doors slid shut, her momentum nearly causing her to slam into the opposite wall. She plopped into her seat, catching her breath. "You were right, Rock," Jasmine said. "Very little dust on the doors. I'm impressed. You notice everything."

"You owe me five hardtack bars, booger brains," Nugget said to his brother.

"I'll give you five boogers," Pickaxe grumbled. He pressed a finger over one nostril and tipped his head up, aiming to shoot a nose rocket at Nugget.

Rock rolled his eyes as the brothers wrestled each other to the floor. "Just as I thought," he said. "Now, how many specks of dust per square centimeter were there?"

Jasmine raised pleading eyebrows to Strike. "Is he joking?" she asked.

Strike burst out laughing. "Welcome to my world."

"What's so funny?" Rock asked. "Or is that a sad sort of laugh based on the fact that you owe me ten more hardtack bars?"

"We never shook on it."

Rock flipped through his notebook to a page marked "Hardtack Bars Strike Owes Me," and changed the number to thirty-two. The next page was a list titled "Ways of Tricking Yourself into Believing that Hardtack Bars Aren't Disgusting."

The rest of that page was blank.

The tram shuddered and then picked up speed, moving down the tracks. Rock studied the sweaty little girl, who had already caught her breath. "How'd you get to be so fast?"

Jasmine scrunched her mouth into a crinkled line. "I don't want to talk about it."

"Why?" Rock asked. "It's incredible. You're faster than Strike. Maybe even TNT. Perhaps whoever trained you could train— Ow!"

Strike jabbed Rock with another elbow. "Her trainer

was probably Torch," he whispered.

"Ah," Rock said. "Right." He shifted uncomfortably in his seat. "Let's get back to game day preparations, then."

Jasmine looked down, shuffling through Rock's stack of gameplay notes. Not meeting anyone's eyes, she quietly sniffled and wiped away tears as she handed the next sheet to Rock.

The Miners stared at each other in silence. Rock tried to start up the strategy session once more, but he kept on petering out at the sound of Jasmine's weeping. Finally, he cleared his throat. "Maybe we've gone over enough for now. Let's take a break."

Strike's mind turned to Torch and the curse he had supposedly brought onto his old team. An eerie shiver went up his spine as he watched Jasmine out of the corner of his eye, wondering if the Torch's Curse had latched on to the Miners, its shadow following them into today's game.

When the Miners ran out of the tunnel into Neutron Stadium, the thunderous boos crashed down like a massive cave-in. Strike had played here many times over his four-year career, but the raw hatred was something he never got used to. Fans in the front rows pelted the Miners with trash, hardtack bars, even rocks. This was technically illegal and could get a fan ejected, but the Blackguard security officers weren't doing anything to stop it. One guy in a black jumpsuit even joined in, hurling a stone right at Strike's head. It was a good thing that they did no damage to the impervious Ultrabot suits, but the barrage constantly triggered warning lights inside the helmets' heads-up displays, making the salvos hard to ignore.

The two teams met at the fifty-meter line. It took a full five minutes for the armored refs to quiet the fans down enough to go through their pregame routine. The head referee, decked out in full body armor and a stainless steel helmet, signaled for the clear impactanium barriers to go up, protecting the crowd from the action on the field. He motioned everyone in. "You all know the rules," he said, screaming to make himself heard over the crowd noise. "I want a clean game, no penalties. Score often, and score a lot."

Strike stuck out a closed fist for White Lightning to tap, the traditional way for captains to start a game. But the Neutron in Fusion's old number 9 suit barely looked up. White Lightning raised a fist and gave the barest of taps before quickly shuffling away. Strike stared at White Lightning's back, wondering why he wouldn't even meet Strike's gaze.

It was almost as if he was hiding something.

Someone punched Strike's chest plate, making him flinch. "Hey," TNT said over the Miners' helmet comm. "You okay?"

"Yeah," Strike said. "Let's go."

The crowd's roar ratcheted back up as the Neutrons lined up to receive the kickoff. Neutron Nation was in full effect today, almost everyone in the stands decked out in the bright red of North Pole Colony. Strike raced forward toward the Ultraball, swinging his leg with all the might his suit could provide, the steel ball rocketing off his boot like it had been shot from a missile launcher. The ball soared, looking like it might even hit the roof of the cavern, a hundred meters above. A perfect kick, leaving plenty of time for the Miners to sprint down the field.

TNT led the Miners, three steps ahead of everyone else. He threw himself into one of Neutron Stadium's slingshot zones, accelerating to hyperspeed before blasting out the other side. His aim dead-on, TNT exploded into one of the defenders like a supercharged tank, blasting the Neutron backward.

Strike let out a scream as he smashed into the Neutrons' crackback 2, Ion Storm, with a metallic clang so loud it reverberated throughout the stadium. But Ion Storm was better than Strike had remembered, staying on his feet to hold his ground as they wrestled for position.

The Neutron ball carrier, hiding behind Ion Storm, jab-stepped left. In the split second that Strike had taken to process the guy's move, Ion Storm shifted his weight and threw Strike off balance. With a burst of speed, the ball carrier crashed into both of them, trying to muscle his way through. Miners and Neutrons came crashing in, piling up in a scrum.

Directly on top of Strike, Ion Storm flipped his visor to clear, his lips pulled back in a menacing growl. He drew back a gloved fist and punched Strike's left shoulder so hard that Strike could almost feel it through the indestructible armor. "Deathstrike!" he yelled. He slammed another punch into Strike's shoulder. And then another. And another.

Deathstrike? The word stabbed fear into Strike's chest as he tried to wriggle out from under the pile. As more players slammed in, fighting each other for the ball, another Neutron pushed in to pin Strike's arms down. Ion Storm whaled away at Strike's shoulders, each blow faster and harder than the one before. Panic mounted in Strike as everything closed in on him, conjuring terrifying images of a coffin slamming shut over his face. Then his frenzy turned to shock when he realized where Ion Storm was targeting every single one of his punches.

Does he know my secret?

When the refs finally came in to break things up, Ion Storm grabbed Strike and stared at him through his clear visor, his mouth twisted into an evil grin. He gave Strike a hard shove before walking to his huddle.

The Neutrons went four and out on their first series, turning it over to the Miners on the fifty-meter line. The first play out of scrimmage, the Miners lined it up in a slingshot V formation, with TNT far backfield, ready to be accelerated into rocket speed by Rock and Pickaxe. Strike took a long glance at a slingshot zone—hopefully enough to make the Neutrons think a long bomb was coming. "Mercury eighty-six!" he yelled. "Mercury eighty-six fireball!" The audible was a fake, but two of the Neutrons seemed to bite, shifting toward the slingshot zone.

Rock dropped back to where TNT was, and both of them sprinted toward the line, Rock leading the charge as TNT's blocker. Nugget hiked the ball to Strike just before Rock crossed the line of scrimmage, cannonballing into one of the Neutron defenders with a metallic crunch.

TNT hurdled over everyone and streaked toward the slingshot zone. His defender was with him every step, both of them bumping and shoving for position. TNT hit the slingshot zone first and boomed out the other side, hurtling into the sky. The defender hit the zone only a split second later, but with the burst of slingshot speed, TNT was already meters ahead. "I'm open!" he yelled into the helmet comm.

Safely in the pocket behind Nugget and Pickaxe, Strike wound up for the big throw. His heads-up display targeted onto TNT, flashing green. Every cell in his body screamed to let it fly, just like the old days. But he pulled the ball down, juked left, and spun under an oncoming defender. Rock had crept into the midfield, and Strike dumped it to him.

The Neutrons converged on the Miners' rocketback 2, quickly corralling him. Meltdown rammed his shoulder into Rock's chest plate, knocking him backward. Radioactive smashed in next, slamming both Rock and Meltdown to the turf.

The play was over, with a short gain just like the Miners had planned. Strike jogged forward toward the pile. But someone cracked into him from the side, lifting him off his feet. The defender held him high in a bear hug and then threw him to the turf.

Disoriented, Strike looked up to see Ion Storm's sly grin right above him. Another Neutron shielded them from the ref's view. *I'm gonna bury you*, Ion Storm mouthed before slamming a punch into Strike's shoulder. "Deathstrike!"

TNT came barreling in, knocking Ion Storm clean off him. Flipping his visor to clear, TNT offered Strike a hand. "You okay?"

Breathing hard, it took Strike several long moments to respond. There it was again—the word "Deathstrike." It had to be a stupid scare tactic, but it sure was accomplishing its goal.

"Fine. Just got surprised, that's all." As the Miners walked back to the huddle, Strike closed his eyes, trying to tamp down his panic.

The Miners' surprise short-passing game mostly

worked, allowing Strike to dump the ball off to TNT, Rock, or even one of his crackbacks, constantly chipping away with unpredictable plays for fifteen meters here, twenty meters there. Even when they didn't score within four downs, that forced the Neutrons to start their drives from deep in their own territory. Slowly, the Miners built up a lead, holding on to it even as momentum switched from team to team.

The Neutrons, especially Ion Storm, never let up on Strike. They began to jam the line, double- or even triple-teaming him, which allowed the Miners to score if Strike was able to get the ball off quickly enough. But when he didn't, he got sacked, the Neutron crackbacks both piling on top of him, smashing gloved fists into his shoulders. The cheap shots came fast and furious, rabbit punches and haymakers and kill shots, all aimed at his shoulders.

In the past, Strike had gotten used to the Neutrons' physical playing style and was able to tune out the intimidation. But his panic kept creeping up on him, mounting with each play. Twice, he threw desperation passes into slingshot zones so that they'd accelerate through, blasting all the way downfield to a streaking TNT. But both passes were intercepted and returned all the way back for touchdowns. After each pick-seven, the Neutron crackbacks made a beeline for Strike, viciously tackling him,

Fuel Rod holding Strike down as Ion Storm whaled away at Strike's shoulders.

When the whistle blew to end the first half, the Miners jogged off the field toward their locker room, the impactanium barriers separating the stands from the playing field lowered for halftime. A rock the size of a fist clanged off Strike's helmet, sending warning lights flashing in his heads-up visor.

Strike had endured a punishing half of Ultraball. His brain raging into a red fury, he roared. He grabbed the small rock someone had thrown at him and cocked back his arm, ignoring the pain of his suit pinching at his shoulders. With a monstrous bellow, he heaved his arm forward with all the might of his Ultrabot suit behind it.

The fans screamed in terror. Spectators jumped out of their seats, scrambling over each other to scatter under benches and into aisles.

At the last moment, TNT smacked Strike's gloved hand, knocking the stone out, sending it to the turf. "What the frak are you doing?" TNT asked. He flipped his visor to clear, his eyes wild with anger and confusion.

Strike seemed to observe himself from somewhere near the roof, floating way above the turf. It was as if someone had taken over his body and willed it to do the unthinkable. He had been aiming the throw at the far back wall of the stadium, so the stone wouldn't have hit anyone. But the mass panic might have caused a stampede. People could have gotten trampled. And the Miners would have been disqualified, putting them in a serious hole against the rival Neutrons.

The other Miners swarmed Strike, rushing him toward the tunnel leading to the locker room. More and more trash and rocks pelted them. The boos came raining down even harder, the quaking rumbles vibrating all the way through Strike's Ultrabot suit.

The Miners finally got into the tunnel. The door slid shut behind them. The Miners clicked out of their Ultrabot suits, Strike quicker than everyone else in his desperation to escape his claustrophobic coffin.

TNT grabbed Strike's jumpsuit, yanking him around so they were face-to-face. "What is with you today?"

It was all Strike could do to not to reach for his left shoulder, aching with a mix of real and phantom pain. "I hate the Neutrons," he finally said. "I hate them so frakkin' much."

"The best way to get back at them is to beat them," TNT said. "Let's add some long bombs into the plan."

"The short game has been working surprisingly well," Rock said. "We are up by seven."

"Yeah. But if I get open, jam it into me," TNT said. "Let it fly and I'll go up and get it. Just like the old days." He sat forward, expectantly awaiting Strike's answer.

Strike could hardly look at his teammates. He had let

everyone down in such a big way. He was supposed to be their quarterback, their coach, the general manager. He was failing in every role. "I'm sorry," he said in a whisper.

"Don't be sorry," TNT said. "Be mad. Gather up that anger and turn it loose against the Neutrons."

"That is one area in which they're handily beating us," Rock said. "They're punishing you during each play, even if it means that they give up extra meters. I thought it made no sense at first." He cocked his head. "But now I realize how smart that strategy is."

"Rock has a point," Pickaxe said. He smacked a fist into his open palm. "We have to hit White Lightning, hard. Like Boom did last year." He nudged his brother. "Turn us loose, Coach. We'll pile-drive White Lightning's head straight into the turf. Bury him, like the Neutrons have been doing to you."

"Let me and Pickaxe whale away at everyone," Nugget said. "We're your enforcers. We gotta make them pay for what they've been doing to you."

"We all want part of that," TNT said. "We have to show the Neutrons that if they pull that stuff on you, the Miners will torture them."

Pickaxe punched a locker. "Payback."

Even after all the punishment he'd taken, a nagging sensation ate away at Strike. White Lightning had suffered so much, the butt of the moon after his humiliation at the hands of Boom. No one deserved to be beaten down even further than that. And now that Strike thought about it, White Lightning was the sole Neutron who hadn't thrown a single cheap shot at him.

But Ultraball was war. He couldn't afford to be soft. He slowly nodded.

"All right," Pickaxe said, slapping a high five with his brother. "Down in the trenches, we're gonna get rough. Ugly."

"Blitz three, mob swarm?" Rock suggested.

"Now that's what I'm talking about," Nugget said.

TNT raised his fists, swinging away. "Let's go smack the Neutrons in their frakkin' faces."

And they did. The first play of the second half, the Miners sent in an atomic wave blitz, hitting White Lightning from three different directions, smashing him to the turf. The Miners turned up the heat on the Neutrons' quarterback, always having at least two players chase him relentlessly. He did make some plays, but he also made mistakes. The Neutrons ended their first three possessions with a White Lightning fumble, a White Lightning touchdown throw, and a turnover on downs when Pickaxe and Nugget timed the count perfectly on fourth down, Nugget whipping Pickaxe over the defenders to smash into White Lightning just as he picked up the ball.

Forced to use their one and only time-out of the game, the Neutrons made adjustments to give White Lightning more protection. But the Miners kept up the furious pace, doubling down on their single-minded focus of torturing White Lightning. For a while, he kept his composure, but every time the Miners batted down one of his passes, forced him into throwing an interception, or stripped the ball out of his hands, White Lightning got more flustered. As the game went on, White Lightning's play faltered.

With just twenty seconds to go, the game was tied, 77–77, and the Miners had the ball on the fifty-meter line, fourth down. Inside the huddle, TNT slapped Strike's chest plate. "Now we push in the dagger," he said through the helmet comm. "Check this out." He stood up and pointed high into the stands with two fingers extended on each hand. "Play of the century, part two!" Turning to White Lightning, he smacked his butt at the Neutron in red.

The stadium announcer caught on right away, his voice booming across the arena. "TNT is signaling for a repeat of the play that ended White Lightning's career with the Saladin Shock in the most embarrassing way possible. What do you think, folks? One-on-one, Strike versus White Lightning?"

A chant started up throughout the stands. "One-on-one! One-on-one!" Everyone was on their feet, screaming, out for blood.

Strike ran over to TNT, pulling his arms down. "Stop.

We don't have to embarrass White Lightning. Let's just play."

"What is the frakkin' matter with you?" TNT said. "We have a chance for a kill shot. You can beat White Lightning one-on-one with your eyes closed. It'd be a sure thing."

"TNT has a point," Rock said. "A normal play might or might not be successful. But if you could make White Lightning go one-on-one, you'd almost surely beat him for a score."

"Yeah, but . . ." White Lightning might be a hated Neutron now, but he was the only Neutron who hadn't thrown a single dirty shot at Strike the entire game. He could have easily joined in, but he hadn't stooped to his teammates' level.

White Lightning had been the laughingstock of the entire league last year, cut by the Shock after he had been beaten one-on-one by Boom and cried afterward. No one deserved to live through that humiliation again.

"No," Strike said. "Everyone line it up, slant fifty-six red."

"A frakkin' slant?" TNT said. "Not another short pass. We might get stuffed way short of the end zone. Air it out long. We'll catch them totally off guard. I'll rocket out of a slingshot zone and go up and get it."

"Slant fifty-six red," Strike repeated. "You'll have all sorts of room to dodge and juke on your way to a score.

And at least one slingshot zone should be wide open for you to launch yourself through."

The announcer kept up his chatter. "Can you believe this? Just over one year ago, White Lightning experienced the worst embarrassment of his life, at the hands of Boom. Will history repeat itself, this time with White Lightning punished by Strike?"

"I like TNT's thinking," Rock said. "A one-on-one play, you versus White Lightning, is sure to result in a touchdown. A short pass might, especially if the Neutrons leave the slingshot zones unguarded, but—"

"No," Strike said. "Now line it up."

"Going one-on-one is the smart thing to do."

"I said, line it up!" Strike stomped his way back to the ball, waving his Miners into position. He stood a few steps away from the line of scrimmage, waiting impatiently as Nugget slowly took his spot over the Ultraball. The crowd was against him. His teammates were against him. But they'd win this game without embarrassing White Lightning again.

TNT took his spot by Strike's side, shaking his head. Even though his visor was flipped to reflective mode, Strike knew there was annoyance all over his face.

Focusing on Nugget and the Ultraball, Strike put up his hands. "Hut. Hut!" The ball whipped into his hands. Strike backpedaled just three steps before lasering the ball to TNT, who was racing forward into the slot. It clanged into TNT's gloved hands a split second before a Neutron crashed into him, sending him careening toward Strike.

TNT had almost broken the tackle when another Neutron hurdled over Pickaxe and smashed in. As TNT went down, he flipped the ball in desperation toward Strike.

The Ultraball flew high, to Strike's left. He leapt up, twisting as he desperately stretched to the max. His shoulders screamed in pain. The ball seemed to float over his fingertips, but then it snapped into place, his glove electromagnets sucking it in. Kicking off someone's head, Strike jumped over two defenders and landed back to the turf. A slingshot zone was ten meters in front of him. He charged ahead, accelerating to top speed.

The Neutrons came in hot. Meltdown raced toward Strike on an intercept course and threw himself into the air. The two of them hit the slingshot zone at the same time, blasting out the other side, locked together as one. Meltdown slammed fist after fist into Strike's gloves and helmet, but Strike curled up into the fetal position to protect the ball. They slammed to the ground at the twenty-meter line and bounced as they slid toward the end zone. Meltdown tried to wrap Strike up to end the play, but Strike crunched an elbow into the Neutron's visor to break free. He popped to his feet and raced forward, leaping for the goal line.

But he nearly whipped into the turf when Meltdown snagged his ankle. Meltdown heaved backward with a massive pull. Crawling, fighting, punching, Strike fought for every last centimeter. Just as another defender barreled in, Strike collapsed over the goal line, slamming the ball into the end zone.

As the thousands of Neutrons fans in red groaned and swore, the other Miners raced in, jubilantly chest-bumping and high-fiving Strike. "Way to make it interesting," TNT said. He flipped his visor to clear, a grin on his face. "Sorry I didn't trust you. I should have known you wanted to make the big play yourself."

"Yeah," Strike said with a dumb smile. "Just like I planned." He fought back the claustrophobia pressing in all around him and punched a fist into the air. He bellowed out a primal roar. They'd done it. They'd beaten the hated Neutrons. His teammates launched into a series of sky-high, double-twisting backflips, and he joined in with them, not caring one bit about the fans showering them with boos.

TNT flipped him the Ultraball, pointing up at the giant Meltdown Gun etched into the center of the high ceiling—the Neutrons' team logo. "Smash the gun."

Strike laughed maniacally, trying to hide the fact that he no longer had the confidence to make a throw as long as that, not with any accuracy. He drop-kicked the Ultraball, sending it cracking into the impactanium barrier separating the field from the fans, and then turbo butt-slapped a surprised TNT.

After the Miners' touchdown celebration, the two teams lined it up for the customary postgame fist bumps. White Lightning was in the front of the line, and he slowly approached Strike, looking down at the turf. "Thanks for not making me go one-on-one," he mumbled. "I owe you big-time."

Strike nodded. "Thanks for not throwing any cheap shots at me today."

White Lightning turned to leave. Strike almost put a hand on his shoulder to stop him, to try to console him. Everyone was exhausted after an Ultraball game, but White Lightning looked like he hadn't slept in weeks. The bags under his eyes were heavy and dark. His face was pale. Like death.

As White Lightning trudged away, Strike tried to harden himself against the pathetic sight. *Ultraball is war*, he thought. But pity kept on nagging away at him.

He startled when a big guy in a red jumpsuit tapped his shoulder. "This is from Mr. Zuna," the guy said. He handed over a piece of paper folded in half, then stepped away to wait.

Strike looked to the others, pausing before he opened the note. It read:

Your Ultrabot suit is getting tight. You'll be forced to retire soon. I have a solution.

Keep this under wraps and come alone, or the deal is off.

Frozen, Strike remained stone-still in a mixture of shock and horror.

Raiden Zuna knew his secret.

"You okay?" TNT asked him. "What does Zuna want?"

Strike stared dumbly at the ground. He reached for his left shoulder, unable to tell if the aching pains were real, or just in his imagination. He could still play in top form. Or near it, at least. But how long would that last?

"Strike?" Rock and the others crowded around their quarterback, their coach, their leader. Rock's voice lowered to a whisper. "Is it about Boom?" He patted his side, where his prized possession was safely hidden: the phone Boom had given him last year, just in case of absolute emergencies. "Should I call her?"

"No," Strike hissed, snapping out of his trance. "Stop looking for excuses."

"I know," Rock said. "I just . . ." He swallowed down a lump. "I'd give up anything to see her again. Even an Ultrabowl title."

Ultrabowl title, Strike thought. His teammates' entire futures rode on his shoulders.

If he failed . . .

He shook his head. *I have to get back to playing in top form.*

Even though he knew that it might be the stupidest decision he would ever make, Strike looked at the big guy in red and nodded.

RESULTS, WEEK 2

Miners	**84**
Neutrons	77

Molemen	**91**
Explorers	70

Beatdown	**63**
Flamethrowers	56

Shock	**56**
Venom	42

STANDINGS, WEEK 2

	Wins	**Losses**	**Total Points**
Molemen	2	0	168
Neutrons	1	1	182
Miners	1	1	154
Beatdown	1	1	147
Flamethrowers	1	1	140
Explorers	1	1	133
Shock	1	1	119
Venom	0	2	70

THE OFFER

Strike followed behind the bodyguard in red, walking up a long set of stairs leading to the North Pole Stadium skyboxes. The other Miners had pleaded for him to not go, but there was no way he could miss a once-in-a-lifetime opportunity to extend his playing career. Making some sort of deal with Zuna was making a deal with the devil. This was the man who had nearly taken over Taiko Colony last year, with every intention of cratering it. But Strike would do anything to win an Ultrabowl title for his teammates.

They stopped at a pitch-black door recessed into the wall. The bodyguard pressed a button on a control panel, and the door clicked open. "Mr. Zuna will see you now," he said. "I'll escort you back down after your meeting."

Strike edged toward the door. His breath caught. He'd heard about places like this back on Earth, throne rooms adorned in gold and silver, crystal chandeliers hanging from the ceiling, catching the light and throwing rainbow patterns across the room.

"Hello, Strike," Zuna said. He stood up from behind a wood desk, its surface polished to an oily finish, representations of wild animals carved into the legs. "What do you think?" He waved a hand across his surroundings. "It's not my best suite, but it's hard to beat the view."

Strike stepped forward toward the panoramic window separating them from the stands. His eyes widened as he took in the sight of North Pole Stadium. He could see everything from here. There were even displays mounted near the ceiling that projected zoomed-in close-ups.

"Nothing but the best for the North Pole Neutrons," Zuna said. "This is all due to our Ultrabowl wins. Every one of the Neutrons is set for life." He shook his head. "No one remembers the losers."

"Like your Neutrons?" Strike said. "Remind me, who just won this game?"

"Ultraball is a war," Zuna said. "This is only one battle. We'll end this season with a title. Just like last year."

Heat rose through Strike's head as something clicked into place. This might have been the exact spot where Zuna had aimed his Meltdown Gun at Boom last year and pulled the trigger. And now Zuna was taunting him about it?

He spun on his heels and stormed toward the door, but Zuna called out. "Sit, Strike. Your Ultrabot suit is getting tight. You panic when you think about outgrowing it, about your Ultraball career being over. And for good reason. It won't be long before the suit won't seal up around you anymore. Maybe you have months. But it might only be weeks."

Strike started to deny it all, but it was useless. "How did you know?" he asked.

"Because it's what happened to Chain Reaction," Zuna said.

Strike took a step back, trying to process the information. Slowly, the pieces were starting to come together. "So that's why you replaced him," he said. "Chain Reaction outgrew his suit over the off-season."

"Always one step behind," Zuna said. "Chain Reaction started to outgrow his suit two years ago. Think, Strike. Why would I ask you here?"

Strike's head felt like it was overheating, shorting out. Why *had* Zuna asked him here? It had to do with the Ultrabot suit tightening around Strike, just as it had around Chain Reaction—

Strike jolted, the realization smashing into him like a blitzing crackback. He hardly dared to ask the question. "You have a way to enlarge a suit?" That was impossible, given how technologically advanced the Ultrabot suits were. They were so complicated that no one on the moon fully understood how they worked. But Strike held his breath. Maybe Zuna, with all his money, had found a way to make the impossible happen.

"Lucky for Chain Reaction, he was a North Pole Neutron," Zuna said. "Neutron Nation is unstoppable. North Pole Colony's technology is unparalleled."

Without thinking, Strike blurted out, "What do you want in return for enlarging my suit?"

Zuna smiled. "I'm glad we understand each other. I give you something, you give me something. I'm not even asking for much." He raised a shoulder in a casual shrug. "All I want is Boom's location."

Caught off guard by the mention of his former star rocketback, Strike struggled to remain stoic. He shrugged back. "She's dead."

"Don't insult my intelligence," Zuna said. "You didn't fool me one bit with all that talk last year about her dying somewhere on the Dark Side, back among her filthy people. Of course that's what you'd do, telling the world of her death so that I wouldn't come after her. No, she's still alive." He pointed to a plush padded chair. "Sit."

"No thanks." Strike stood rigidly, trying not to give anything away. Wraith's words echoed through his head: *Boom needs you. She's safely hidden away, gathering an army.*

"Boom is working behind the scenes with Wraith,"

Zuna said. "They're the ones who stole nuclear weapon components from North Pole Colony. I'm sure of it. Eliminating Boom is a matter of national security. It's your duty to turn her in."

Strike remained silent, his fingers fidgeting. *That's kind of what Governor Katana said*, he thought.

"You might not know exactly where she is," Zuna said. "But you do know how to get in contact with her. Now, I know what you're thinking. You're wondering how guilty you'd feel, trading Boom's life so that you can play another Ultraball season or two. But that's not the right way to think about it. Choosing the right course of action would save lives. You'd be brave. Heroic. Helping to keep the moon safe from anarchists—anarchists who are looking to build nuclear weapons. Being able to extend your Ultraball career? That's simply a bonus."

"She didn't steal those nuclear components. She's dead."

Zuna leaned forward, locking eyes with Strike. He pressed his palms into the desk as if he was preparing to crush it. "It's your patriotic duty to turn her in. The Dark Siders are the biggest threat humanity has ever faced. Even more dangerous than the terrorists who caused Earthfall."

"Terrorists?" Strike blinked in confusion. "You mean the Earthfall Eight?"

"What do they teach you these days?" Zuna asked, shaking his head. "The Earthfall Eight may have been the ones to push the nuclear launch buttons. But Earthfall would never have happened if the radical insurgents behind the scenes had been stopped." He raised his right hand with a firm solemnity. "I'm offering you the chance to be a hero for the United Moon Colonies, as well as to extend your Ultraball career. It's a no-brainer. Turn in the terrorists."

Although Zuna seemed to honestly believe what he was saying, this business about the Dark Siders being terrorists was ridiculous. All they wanted was to be left alone. But one thing was true: the man wearing the Governor's Star of North Pole Colony was offering Strike a once-in-a-lifetime opportunity. This wasn't just about Strike extending his Ultraball career. The futures of all his teammates depended on him leading the Miners to an Ultrabowl title. He thought about the phone Boom had put in Rock's pocket, with instructions to only use it in a dire emergency.

Was it time to make the call?

But then, Strike thought about what Rock would say to all of this. So many things didn't make sense. Why would Zuna help Strike, if that meant strengthening the Neutrons' biggest rival? Something wasn't right.

Strike shook his head.

"You disappoint me, Strike," Zuna said. He stood up, motioning toward the door. "I expected more out of you. Get out."

"With pleasure," Strike said. He stormed out, swearing at himself under his breath. He couldn't believe he'd even agreed to listen to the most evil man on the moon.

As Strike reached the door, Zuna called out, "Remember, Strike. There is nothing more important than national security. Boom is an enemy of the state. Aiding and abetting an enemy of the state is an act of treason." When Strike turned to look back, Zuna's fiery gaze burned holes into him. "The penalty for treason is death."

The bodyguard yanked Strike out the door and manhandled him toward the stairs.

THE GUARDIAN

INSIDE THEIR ULTRABALL tram, Strike tried to listen to all the information and data that Rock was throwing at the Miners about their week-three opponent, the Kamar Explorers. The Miners had prepared harder than ever, to the point that Strike wondered if he had pushed everyone too far. Even Jasmine, sitting at the end of one row of seats, looked tired as she furiously scribbled down everything Rock said.

He startled as Rock waved a hand in his face. "Strike?" Rock said. "So, what do you think?"

Strike's eyes darted around. Everyone was watching him, waiting. "Uh. Yeah. Definitely," he said.

Rock's head tilted to the side, an eyebrow rising in question. "I was expecting more of an argument. But I'm glad you agree. Stretching the field by throwing more long bombs to TNT will be a great help to our offense."

"What? No, that's not what I meant," Strike said.

His other eyebrow going up, Rock cleared his throat. "So, when I asked if we should go back to having more long passes in our game plan and you said yes, I was misinterpreting you?"

"Yes. No. What? Don't try to confuse me."

"It seemed like a simple question," Rock said. He looked around. "Am I wrong?"

"No," Jasmine said. She took out a notebook and read from it. "You asked Strike about throwing more long passes, going back to game plans that worked so well back when TNT—"

"No one likes a wise guy," Strike said. Despite his annoyance, he grinned at Jasmine. It was funny to watch her scramble as she tried to keep up with Rock's never-ending requests.

"I don't know about that," Pickaxe said. "Mini Rock is okay by me." He went to give Jasmine a friendly slug on the shoulder, but she ducked away so quickly that Pickaxe whiffed, his missed punch making him lurch.

Nugget cackled with glee at his brother. "I'd make a joke about you being slow, but the joke tells itself— Ow!"

He winced as Pickaxe wheeled around and slugged his shoulder.

"Now who's slow?" Pickaxe asked with a smile. The tram shuddered, curving hard on its way into Kamar station, sending Pickaxe off balance. He nearly toppled over, but Jasmine jumped to scurry in behind, propping him up before he could fall.

Narrowing his eyes, Pickaxe studied her. "You're like a rocket. A teeny tiny nitro rocket."

"Good one," Rock said. He opened his notebook to a page titled "Excellent Nicknames" and scrawled in "Nitro," "Rocket," and "Nitro Rocket."

"All right, everyone," Strike said. "Let's go unload. Big game ahead." As always, there was a crowd of fans gathered in the station, waiting to cheer on the team. Most everyone was dressed in the blue jumpsuits of Taiko Colony, but there were plenty of other colors dotted throughout the area. He pressed a button and the tram door slid back.

A loud cheer erupted as Strike stepped out, smiling and waving to everyone. He'd always loved these moments in the past, but now it seemed more important than ever to savor them. Who knew which one would be his last?

Then he caught sight of a blur to his left and all hell broke loose. Someone was barreling through the crowd, heading straight at Strike, something glinting in his hand. The attacker slammed into the Miners, but two people had thrown themselves in front of Strike to absorb the blow. They all hit the ground, Strike's head cracking down hard. All the air exploded out of his lungs, a searing pain ripping through his chest. He couldn't breathe. All he could do was curl into the fetal position as the station erupted into a mass of screams and panic. Two bodyguards threw themselves on top of him, the pressure threatening to crush him.

A siren cut through the air, an amplified voice blaring over the station loudspeaker. "Everyone, get down! If you are up, we will put you down." Sharp crackles of electricity sparked, the sound of electrostun weapons popping in Strike's ears. The mass hysteria ratcheted up. Strike couldn't see a thing, but horrible images tore through his head. He closed his eyes tight, trying to hide from it all.

"Get away from Strike, you lunatic!" Pickaxe yelled.

"I'm protecting him, you fool," someone said. "He's in danger. Now let me talk to him before the Blackguards come."

In his confusion, Strike squeezed his eyes even harder, concentrating as he tried to place the familiar voice. "Wraith?" he croaked.

Bodies slowly unpiled from Strike. He cracked an eye, spotting Wraith right above him. "Someone in a blue jumpsuit tried to kill you," she whispered.

"What are you doing in Kamar Colony?" Strike asked.

"Boom asked me to keep you safe at all costs." She stole a glance over her shoulder. "I can't always be around you, though. Zuna is watching me constantly. You have to be smarter about staying safe. The rebellion army needs you." She pushed off and sprinted away.

The tumult around the station died down, the yells and screams slowly morphing into moans. Strike sat up, a sharp pain at his side. His eyes widened as he caught sight of Nugget and Pickaxe huddled together over TNT. His star rocketback 1 was on the ground, writhing, holding his gut. "TNT," Strike said. "Are you okay?"

Rock shook his head. "We need to get him to Salaam Hospital."

"I'm fine," TNT said through gritted teeth. His hand was pressed over his stomach, a red spot staining his jumpsuit.

"Holy frak," Strike said. He moved toward TNT, but his friend rolled to face the other way.

"Just give me a second," TNT said. He let out a guttural groan. "Help me get inside my Ultrabot suit and I'll be good to go."

"You're bleeding," Rock said. He carefully moved TNT's hand aside, peering at the wound. "It doesn't look like the cut is deep. But you definitely shouldn't play."

"Get me into my frakkin' suit," TNT said. "I just need to be breathing, and the Ultrabot suit will do the rest for me."

"You can barely sit up," Rock said. He looked to Strike. "I don't think you should let him play. He'll hurt himself further."

"What happened?" Strike asked. He leaned in to stare at the bloody spot on TNT's jumpsuit.

"He and Wraith jumped in to protect you when that guy ran at you with a knife," Nugget said. "If it hadn't been for the two of them . . ." He paused, nearly choking on his words.

A crowd had gathered around them, onlookers asking if they could help. The circle tightened, everyone too close. Strike held up his hands. "Everyone back up," he said. "Give us some space."

"I have a phone," a guy in a gold jumpsuit said. "Should I call Salaam Hospital?"

"No," TNT said. He winced in pain. "Don't take me there. I have to play. We'll forfeit otherwise."

"You can't play," Rock said quietly. "We need to get you to the hospital."

"We can't afford the hospital," TNT said.

Strike and Rock looked at each other in silence. Salaam Hospital was only for the rich. Even the Miners couldn't pay for a trip to the hospital.

"I'm telling you, I'm fine," TNT said. He tried to sit up but doubled back over, his face scrunching in agony. "Call someone from the backup list. We can't forfeit. Go win this one for me."

Rock turned to Strike. "What do we do?"

A million thoughts bounced through Strike's head. He studied TNT, who lay back down, groaning. "We have to get him to the hospital," Strike said. "But will we be able to pay for it?"

As the person who handled the Miners' team finances, Rock strained in thought. After a long pause, he pursed his lips. "I'll have to find a way. Let's get him onto the tram."

"You'll be okay," Strike said, but with no conviction in his voice. "We'll be with you the entire way."

Just as Strike was about to tell the onlooker to call Salaam Hospital, TNT grabbed his wrist. Spasms wracked through TNT, his breathing short and ragged. He locked eyes with his quarterback, his best friend, blinking hard, willing Strike to do what had to be done.

It had been a long time since they had shared a moment like this, where Strike knew exactly what TNT was thinking. Strike had to somehow go on with the game. If he didn't, TNT would never forgive him.

Strike looked toward the guy who was still holding up his phone. "Call the hospital and tell them five of our bodyguards will be bringing TNT in. And then call . . ." He flinched, looking to Rock. "Frak. Tell me that someone on our backup list has a phone. Anyone." But he already knew the answer. Almost no one in Taiko Colony had a phone anymore, much less any kids.

Rock was already shaking his head as he opened his notebook.

"I'll take a tram back to Taiko Colony," Jasmine said. "I'm fast. I'll find whoever you need."

"There's not enough time," Rock said. "The game is going to start in an hour."

"Then we're dead," Strike said. "We have to forfeit."

"Not necessarily," Rock said. He turned to Jasmine. "You can play."

"Me?" The little girl shrank down, looking smaller than ever.

"As you said, you're fast," Rock said. "And your big brother . . . I bet a lot of Torch's knowledge has rubbed off on you."

Jasmine raised her shoulders in a tentative shrug. "He actually got me some time in an Ultrabot suit back when he was quarterbacking the Flamethrowers."

Strike looked at Rock skeptically. "She doesn't know our playbook."

"She does," Rock said. "She's been helping me catalog game data. Her Ultraball IQ is off the charts."

Strike rubbed his chin as he studied the girl. "You think you can do it?"

Jasmine jammed her hands into her jumpsuit pockets. "No way," she said, her face twisted in agony. "What if I screw up? Me and Torch, we're cursed."

"There's no such thing as a curse," Rock said.

"Torch cursed the Flamethrowers for years after he lost that Ultrabowl."

"It was just bad luck that the Flamethrowers were so terrible after that," Strike said.

"That's the very definition of a curse," Jasmine said. She shook her head. "I can't do that to the Miners. No way. I'm not playing."

"What about making up for what Torch did last year?" TNT said in a growl. "You said you'd do anything. And now you're backing out?" He grabbed his side, his hand twitching. "You have to try. Otherwise we'll forfeit."

"We don't have any other options," Rock said. "We need you. Please."

Jasmine looked down at her feet and swore under her breath. Finally, she gave a hesitant nod.

Strike turned to glance at a clock mounted high on the side of Kamar Arena. "Let's go. We have less than an hour to get her up to speed. Everyone unload quick. I have to turn in our new roster to the officials ASAP. Go!"

The Miners flew in action, following Strike's orders.

He caught Jasmine's nervous glance and mustered up a confident smile for her. The pressure would be intense. She'd be the focus of every fan and color commentator, every one of her mistakes and missteps analyzed to death.

Strike turned away with a guilty tinge of relief that it wouldn't be him under the harsh spotlight today.

SCOREBOARD HIGHLIGHTS

THE BIG ROSTER change had been announced five minutes ago, but there was still a buzz in the air. Strike tried to focus on the play they had called for the kickoff return, but the shock of everything that had happened still had him on the verge of a breakdown. Attempted murder. TNT at the hospital, no one even knowing if he'd survive. Jasmine stepping in at the last minute to avoid forfeit. The guy with the knife had disappeared without a trace, not a surprise if Zuna was behind it. The Blackguards in Zuna's pocket might have even been helping the guy. This might have been what Ion Storm had been talking about when he had yelled "Deathstrike" during last week's game.

But it wasn't like Zuna to order a direct attack on Strike's life. Zuna still needed Strike alive if he thought Strike could lead him to Boom. So if Zuna wasn't behind this, who was? A deranged fan? Someone betting heavily on the Neutrons, who wanted to take out their biggest competition?

He jumped and cried out when a fist clanged into his shoulder.

"Game time," Pickaxe said. He pointed to a ref, who was signaling toward Strike. "Thirty seconds to kickoff."

Strike took a deep breath and bit his lip. "Miners together. Let's win this one for TNT. Nitro, you ready?"

There was only silence over the helmet comm.

Strike jogged over to slug Jasmine's shoulder. "Nitro!"

"Oh, right, *I'm* Nitro," she said. "Yes. I'm ready." She paused. "I think. Maybe."

Strike turned away so she wouldn't see the concern on his face. "Everyone else?"

"Ready," Pickaxe and Nugget said.

Strike turned to Rock, who was staring at the scoreboard. "Hey. Did you hear me?"

"What?" Rock whipped his head around, coming out of a fog. "The bottom of the scoreboard. It's bizarre."

"What's bizarre is that kickoff is in twenty seconds and you're staring into space," Strike said. He grabbed Rock's shoulders. "Focus."

"Sorry," Rock said. He raced into position as the Miners set up to receive the kickoff. "Has their new field feature been announced yet?"

"They're still keeping it secret," Strike said. "We'll find out soon enough." Ultraball teams sometimes changed their home field features during the off-season. Waiting until the last second in their home opener to unveil it made for a huge advantage, and the Kamar Explorers were going to milk it today.

"Set up in wedge four," Strike said over helmet comm. A standard kickoff receiving pattern, wedge four would let the Miners adjust to whatever the Explorers tried to surprise them with. Strike tried hard to focus on the game, and not on the fact that just an hour ago, someone had tried to kill him.

A whistle blew, starting the game. The Explorers raced forward, one of them booting the ball high into the air. Strike took a few steps back, getting ready to catch the long kick.

But at the top of its high arc, the ball smacked into a plate fixed to Kamar Arena's low ceiling. An explosion blasted out in a shower of gold sparks. The next thing Strike knew, there were five Ultraballs coming down at him. "What's going on?" he yelled.

"Maybe they're holograms," Rock said.

"Which ball do I go for?" Strike said.

"Second one on the right has the closest expected trajectory," Rock said.

Strike shifted to his right to adjust. "Give me protection." The Miners set up in front of him as a wall of blockers as Strike tried to study both the balls falling toward him and the Explorers racing at them at full speed.

"Wait," Nitro shouted as the five balls arced down. "That's not the real ball!"

Strike barely had time to register what she said before the ball he had been targeting slammed into his chest plate, jolting him backward. It exploded in a cloud of gold sparkles, enveloping him in a mist of crackling static electricity. His sensors went haywire, random digits and warning lights flashing across his heads-up display. A split second later, someone bashed into him, knocking him clear off his feet, slamming him down into the end zone.

Strike rolled away from the Explorers' defender, popping back to his feet, his heads-up display clearing, allowing him to locate the rest of his teammates. Rock and Pickaxe were locked in a struggle with two Explorers defenders, but Nitro was charging down the sideline with the Ultraball, Nugget blocking at her side. An Explorer crashed into Nugget and desperately launched himself at Nitro. Just as the player locked a magnetic glove onto her shoulder plate, she whipped around and smashed a second ball into his visor. They both disappeared as the ball exploded into a fog of sparkling gold dust.

Strike raced toward them, hoping that he could at least throw a helpful block. But by the time he arrived, the shimmering cloud had dissipated, and Nitro was standing in the end zone, holding the real Ultraball against her chest plate. She flipped her visor to clear, half excited and half confused. "I scored?" she said.

Strike raced in to high-five her. "Awesome. Do your touchdown dance."

Nitro raised the Ultraball over her head and tentatively spiked it to the turf.

Pickaxe and Nugget raced in, jumping on top of her, everyone collapsing into a dog pile. "We're gonna have to work on your touchdown celebration," Pickaxe said. "But the way you smashed the fake Ultraball into your defender's face was frakkin' awesome."

"How did you figure out which one was the real Ultraball?" Strike asked.

"The spin," Nitro said. "The others were rotating too slowly. Like they had something sloshing around inside them."

"Clever," Rock said. "Quick thinking."

"Not to mention, you were quick enough to pick up both the real ball and a fake one," Nugget said. "Incredible."

"Your block gave me just enough time to smash that defender but good," Nitro said. She gently patted Nugget's chest plate. "This might actually not be as bad as I thought."

"You're already doing better than Pickaxe," Nugget said. "Pooped his pants during his first game."

Pickaxe's face burned red. "That was four years ago," he said. "When are you going to let that drop?"

"You're the one who let it drop. Right inside your Ultrabot suit." Nugget cackled as he ducked a swipe from Pickaxe.

Strike smiled big at Nitro as they jogged back to kick off the ball for the next play. "Great job. We might have to run a few plays your way."

The others followed Strike back toward where a ref was teeing up the ball—everyone except Rock, who was standing off to one side, staring at the scoreboard.

"Rock," Strike said. "What are you waiting for? Huddle up."

"Sorry," Rock said. "Just a second." He cocked his head, fixated on the scoreboard.

Strike ran over and chucked Rock's arm. "Come on. I need you to focus."

Strike's trusty rocketback 2 stood frozen in place, staring at the scoreboard. Although the play clock ticked down with only twenty seconds to go, Rock remained in place, not saying a word.

Grabbing Rock's arms, Strike jerked him off his feet, hauling him back toward the huddle. "What the frak is up with you?" he asked. "Get your head in the game."

Rock swiveled toward Strike as if snapping out of a trance. "Sorry. Did you see the scoreboard?"

"Yeah, the Neutrons are rolling."

"No, not that," Rock said. "The dots and lines along the bottom."

Strike squinted to where Rock was pointing, using his suit's optical magnification to zoom in. But all he could see was the usual border along all four sides of the scoreboard.

"The dots and short lines," Rock said. "Where the borders usually are. They form patterns. Something is odd."

"Yeah, you," Pickaxe said. He yanked Rock into the huddle.

After a four-and-out defensive stop, the Miners got the ball back on their own seven-meter line. Strike stared long and hard at the plate in the ceiling, the trigger for releasing the exploding balls. "Fake double launcher fly forty-three, stunt slant. On two." The Explorers would think the Miners were running a long play through the middle of the field, where the dummy balls could be released. But they'd actually dump the ball off short. With a bit of luck, Rock might even break a couple of tackles and be off to the races.

The five of them lined up in long bomb formation, setting it up so it'd look obvious to the Explorers how to defend. Strike got set over the ball. "Hut one. Hut!"

Nitro jumped off the line exactly when Strike hiked

the ball, smashing into her defender before cutting and racing toward the center of the field. It was perfect. With a tremendous leap, she vaulted toward the low ceiling, all eyes on her.

Up front, Pickaxe and Nugget grappled with the Explorers' rushers, a shoving match that the brothers were winning. With plenty of time, Strike cocked the ball back for a huge fake to Nitro.

But the defenders weren't biting. Rock had released toward the middle too early, tipping off the play. Lasso, the Explorers' rocketback 2, had cut in at an angle, ready to jump the short throw for an interception.

The play was busted. Strike yanked the ball down and activated his glove electromagnets to full power as he cradled the ball and took off running around the left side.

Caught off guard, the defenders scrambled toward Strike, the Explorers' two crackbacks releasing from Pickaxe and Nugget to roll in Strike's direction. But Strike had a couple of steps on the closest one. His shoulder lowered, he built up a head of steam, taking off in schoolyard mode.

Strike hurdled over a defender who had made a desperate swipe at his legs, almost losing his balance, and turned the corner. He raced upfield, giving the next defender a hard fake, getting him to jump off his feet before ducking under the guy. Another defender was racing toward him from the middle of the field, but Strike had the angle. He pushed his Ultrabot suit to the limit, warning lights flashing on the inside of his visor. His power bar dropped at an alarming rate, going from 92 percent all the way to 88 percent in just a few seconds. The defender threw himself at Strike, but with a sudden juke and a double spin, Strike evaded the tackle.

"Strike, watch out!" Nugget yelled into the helmet comm.

Just as Strike turned to look back upfield, another Shock defender barreled in like a missile. Strike usually would have leapt at full extension, trying to arch around the tackle and fly for the goal line. But with his suit biting into his shoulders, he couldn't risk losing a fumble. He curled up as the guy cannonballed into him.

The defender wrapped Strike up and lifted him off the ground. There was nothing Strike could do but hold on to the ball as the guy turned and carried Strike backward, toward his own end zone. As soon as the guy dumped him over the goal line, it would be a touchdown for the Explorers.

Then he lurched as a blue blur cracked into him and the Explorer. They kept moving toward the Miners' end zone, but the defender had lost momentum. Soon, more gold and blue Ultrabot suits rammed in, crushing Strike to the ground.

At the bottom of the pile, Strike clung on to the Ultraball for dear life, his left shoulder erupting into a firestorm of pain, his panic mounting. Players pancaked on top of him, arms swatting and boots kicking at his chest, trying to make him fumble.

Just when the frenzied need to unclick out of his Ultrabot suit nearly overtook him, a whistle blew. Players slowly got off until he could see where he was: just in front of his own end zone.

Pickaxe reached down to pull Strike to his feet. "That was close," he said. "Nitro barely ran you guys down."

"Thanks," Strike said, nodding to Nitro. "You saved us." He looked behind Nitro to where Rock was standing, his visor set to clear, his face flushed with embarrassment.

"I'm so sorry, Strike," Rock said. "I tipped off the play."

It took everything Strike had to keep his cool, to not blow up in Rock's face. Mistakes happened in games all the time—Strike's hesitation about leaping for the end zone was a big one—but this one was huge. If it hadn't been for Nitro's saving tackle, the lowly Explorers would have had an early score, tying things up. He took a couple of deep breaths, closing his eyes before he spoke. "What the frak happened, Rock?"

Rock turned to the scoreboard. "Those dots and dashes along the border. They're a code of some sort. Dash dot dot dot. Dash dash dash. Dash—"

"You gotta focus," Strike said, grabbing Rock's shoulders. "You're my rocketback 1 today. I can't have my feature back studying the scoreboard like it's a test. Not during the game."

"I'm so sorry," Rock said. "It's just . . ." He screwed up his face, something inside him needing to come out. But he remained quiet, shaking his head.

"Don't be sorry," Strike said, punching Rock's chest plate. "Just concentrate on the frakkin' game."

Strike led his team back into the huddle, but when he stole a glance back at Rock, his rocketback 1 was still studying the scoreboard intently.

After the game, the Miners stood at the middle of the field, signing autographs. Strike always enjoyed hanging out with the fans after a win. And today, it was even sweeter, such a relief to have a solid W in the books, considering the pregame attack and the last-minute roster change. They'd gotten news after the game that TNT was stable and recovering at Salaam Hospital, so Strike let himself breathe easy for a moment while the crowd clamored for the Miners' attention.

As he signed souvenir after souvenir, Strike's thoughts turned to their week-four game against the Flamethrowers. He sure hoped his star rocketback would be back in action for their tough matchup against Torch's old team. But if he wasn't, Nitro was a darn good substitute. He glanced at her, standing a couple steps behind her teammates, overwhelmed by all the attention. Not only had she filled in admirably, but she had shown flashes of brilliance. At times, she had reminded Strike of her brother, with his ability to make things happen.

The Miners hadn't run many plays to her. *Maybe we should have*, Strike thought.

Strike snapped out of his trance when a fan got up in his face. "What the frak is this?" the little boy asked. He shoved a little souvenir ball toward Strike.

"That's gratitude for you," Pickaxe muttered. "We stick around so the fans can get autographs, and then they swear at us? Not cool."

The little boy turned his miniature Ultraball, pointing at the signatures. "Rock messed it up. It's ruined." The corners of his mouth pulled into a despondent frown. Sniffles crept out, threatening to escalate into a full-blown meltdown.

Strike checked out the boy's souvenir. There were four signatures on the ball, but where Rock's usually would have been, there was just a pattern of dots and dashes:

— · · ·   — — —   — — —   — —

Strike threw Rock a dirty glare. "Just sign his ball already."

"Dash," Rock said. "Dash dot dot dot." It was as if his body was there in Kamar Arena, but his mind was far away.

Strike looked off into the distance, groaning as he followed Rock's gaze. "The scoreboard dots again? Give it a rest." He motioned to the little boy. "Give us a second. Shouldn't be long."

Pulling out his notebook, Rock mumbled to himself like Strike wasn't even there. "Long?" he muttered.

The little boy tried to wipe off the marks Rock had made. "Mr. Zuna will never buy it now," he whined. He flinched when Strike shot him a dirty glare.

It wasn't uncommon for fans to get autographs just so they could hock the item. But it never stopped annoying Strike, especially when Zuna was the buyer—Neutron Nation loved to destroy other teams' gear during their fanatical rallies. "Gimme that ball, you rotten jerk," he said.

Yanking it back, the little boy scurried off with the ball carefully tucked away.

"Rock," Strike said. "Hey. Hello?" He snapped his fingers in front of Rock's face, but his friend was lost in thought.

Having grown up with Rock his entire life, Strike knew that once Rock slipped into one of these trances, he might be there for a while. He sidled up next to Rock, trying to see what he was scribbling in his notebook.

It was flipped open to a page marked "Secret Codes," and Rock was dotting his pen all over the page, repeatedly stabbing it. "Long," Rock said again. Then he suddenly bellowed. "Long. That's it!"

Strike flinched at the outburst. As the crowd quieted,

everyone staring at them, Strike yanked at Rock's arm, ushering him away. He huddled down with him, cautiously gripping Rock's shoulder. "Are you okay?" He had seen his friend in deep periods of study before, but this was more intense than ever. Focused on his notebook, Rock's eyes were bugging out, his hands trembling, his lips twitching as he struggled to form words.

Strike pulled Rock even farther away from the confused fans, who were all gawking now. "Seriously, man. You're worrying me." He stared into Rock's eyes, silently transmitting a message to his friend: *Please be okay. We can't afford to take you to Salaam Hospital, too.*

Rock continued to splutter as he dotted all over his notebook. But he finally squeezed his eyes tight and took a couple of deep breaths. When he opened his eyes again, they were full of determination. "I was right. It was a code on the scoreboard, using short dots and long dashes. A coded message. To me."

Strike looked at the turf, trying to hide his dread from Rock. The scoreboard, talking to him through secret coded messages? Rock was hallucinating. It could be the first signs of dust poisoning, the scariest disease on the entire moon. He might be forced to take Rock to Salaam Hospital, no matter if they could pay or not. "What kind of code?" Strike asked, afraid to hear the answer. "And who's it from?"

Rock bent down, crouching to make sure no one could

see. He motioned to Strike, pulling him down low, and held his notebook up.

"What am I looking at?" Strike asked. "There's just a bunch of dots and dashes."

"It's an ancient Earth system of cryptography, called Morse code. It died out a long time ago, but she would have known that I'd recognize it. Look." He pointed to his jottings at the bottom of the page.

Strike sucked in a breath. His eyes darted to Rock as his friend circled the first four decoded letters:

B

O

O

M

RESULTS, WEEK 3

Miners	**84**
Explorers	63

Neutrons	**98**
Flamethrowers	84

Molemen	**70**
Shock	56

Beatdown	**98**
Venom	42

STANDINGS, WEEK 3

	Wins	**Losses**	**Total Points**
Molemen	3	0	238
Neutrons	2	1	280
Beatdown	2	1	245
Miners	2	1	238
Flamethrowers	1	2	224
Explorers	1	2	196
Shock	1	2	175
Venom	0	3	112

ROCK'S SURPRISE

A FEW DAYS later, Rock led Strike toward Taiko Arena, four bodyguards in blue trailing behind them. Even though the attack on Strike had been headline news for every media outlet from the *Lunar Times* to the *SmashMouth Radio Blitz* to the *Touchdown Zone*, no one had identified the suspect. It could have been a deranged fan, as *Lunar-Sports* commentators kept saying.

But the most likely explanation was that Zuna was behind the attack. This hadn't made any sense to Strike until it dawned on him that Zuna hadn't been trying to kill him. The attacker had likely been ordered to hurt one of the Miners, to send a message to Strike about what would happen if he didn't give up Boom. It also felt like no coincidence that the person who had gotten stabbed was TNT—the Miners' star player.

Strike glanced over his shoulder, wondering again if four bodyguards were enough. And wondering once again if he should have accepted Zuna's deal.

"I can't wait to see your face," Rock said. "You're going to be so surprised."

"I don't like surprises," Strike said. "Especially from you. Since when do you surprise me?"

"Ever since Boom's coded message gave us a list of surprise strategies that would have let us run up the score against the Explorers," Rock said. "And a whole lot more, for the rest of the season."

"If it was actually Boom."

"I'm positive it was."

Strike shook his head. "Getting messages to you through hidden codes in the border of a scoreboard is insane."

"How else could she do it?" Rock asked. "Not through the phone she gave me—Zuna would trace the call and pinpoint her location. Sending a note to me through a Dark Sider would put that person in way too much danger, and might lead Zuna right back to her. Plus, a coded message is exactly Boom's style. I bet she got the idea from my notebook."

Strike grabbed Rock's shoulders. "I know how badly

you want to believe that Boom is out there trying to help us. And it sure seemed like brilliant game strategy. But would she really take the huge risk of contacting us?"

"Yes, because she wants to make up for the past." Rock bit his lip. "Just like TNT. And Jasmine. Er, Nitro."

Strike's thoughts turned to TNT, stable and recovering but ordered by the doctors not to play for at least two weeks. Nitro had been great as a sub, but Strike needed his superstar back in action.

"Come on," Rock said. "I can't wait for you to see my idea. Well, it's Boom's idea, actually. It's going to transform our team." Rock led Strike toward Taiko Arena, quickening their pace as they approached the airlock door.

It was both cool and nerve-racking to see his friend so amped up. The last time Rock had been this animated was after last year's Ultrabowl, when he had figured out the intricate plan Boom had pulled off. "Should I be scared or excited?" he asked, holding a hand over the entrance button.

"Excited," Rock said. "Very excited."

Strike motioned to the bodyguards to stay outside during practice. Taiko Arena was the Miners' high-security bastion, the one place on the moon where a Miner could not be touched. Strike pushed the button and the doors slid back with a low rumble. The massive cavern of Taiko Arena slowly came into view. Inside, five people stood at the fifty-meter line. The first three were Pickaxe,

Nugget, and Nitro, all facing each other, doing pre-scrimmage stretches in their blue jumpsuits. The fourth was TNT, sitting on the turf, looking glum, his arm tucked in over where he had been stabbed. The fifth was—

"Fusion?" Strike asked in shock. He jabbed a finger at the boy wearing what must have been a borrowed blue jumpsuit.

"Uh," Fusion said, raising a tentative hand. "Hi?"

"How'd he get in here?" Strike said. "We gotta get him out of here before he steals our secrets." He stopped, studying Rock's look of confusion. "Wait a second. This is the surprise? This is why I hate surprises."

"I don't understand," Rock said, his face crinkled. "Why are you so upset? We have the chance to get one of the greatest Ultraball stars of all time on our team. Fusion could be the game changer we need."

Strike was still trying to process what he was seeing: a longtime rival who had crushed Strike's dream to win an Ultrabowl. Four times in a row.

And then it hit him.

Rock wants to put Fusion in as our new quarterback.

He trembled. *Rock knows that my Ultrabot suit is tightening down on me.* Zuna knew. Maybe everyone knew.

"Strike?" Rock said. "Are you okay?"

"How could you?" Strike's words cracked. Emotions

came crumbling forth in waves of sadness, despair, and anger. "After all we've been through, this is the way my Ultraball career is going to end?"

Rock's eyes widened. "What are you talking about? Replacing you would be crazy. I want to address the weakest link on the team." Taking a deep breath, he sighed long and hard before shaking his head. "For the good of the team, we should replace—"

"Don't be ridiculous," Strike snapped. "I'm not going to replace you. Especially not with Fusion." He jabbed a finger at the little boy, who looked like he wanted to bury his head in the turf. "Fusion is a Neutron. He's the enemy."

"Aha," Rock said. "So you admit it."

"Uh. What did I admit?"

"That I'm the weak link of the team."

"I didn't say that."

"But you did. The obvious assumption would have been that I was suggesting you replace Nitro." Rock turned to Nitro, who was also staring at the turf as if she wanted to stick her head in and bury it. "That's not saying anything about you, Nitro. You played great against the Explorers." Rock beamed at Strike, delighted with himself. "I tricked you."

"I hate tricks even more than surprises," Strike muttered. "Look. I only said that because you made it seem like that's what you were going to say. I don't think you're the weak link. You're solid. Dependable. We'd fall apart without you." Strike shot a stink-eyed glare at Fusion.

The skinny kid quietly shoved his hands into the pockets of his jumpsuit.

"As the general manager of the Miners, it's your duty to field the best team available to maximize chances of winning," Rock said. "Imagine what it'd be like to have a dual threat at quarterback, just like last year with Boom. Fusion isn't as good as Boom at rocketback, but he's an incredible all-around player. We could move him all over the place. We could even play him at crackback. It would befuddle defenses."

As much as Strike hated to admit it, Rock had a point. Last year, Boom's arm had given the Miners a deadly weapon that teams hadn't been able to defend against. Having two quarterbacks on their team could make all the difference.

"Neutrons," Strike muttered. "Fusion might be a spy for Zuna. Did you ever think of that?"

"Zuna cut Fusion," Rock said. "Replaced him with White Lightning."

"Exactly," Strike said. "It's probably some intricate plot, making it look like Fusion is begging for a job. And then, bam! Zuna has his spy planted, ready to crater us at the worst possible moment. Just like last year."

"But I went looking for Fusion, not the other way around."

"It's true," Fusion said. "Two Dark Siders snuck me out of North Pole Colony through one of their tunnel systems."

"There's a hidden hatch behind Taiko Elementary School, not far away from Shinjuku Park," Rock said. "It took a lot of planning to get Fusion here without anyone finding out. Boom laid out such careful instructions within her secret scoreboard message."

Strike threw up his arms in exasperation. "Zuna probably anticipated that you or me would come looking for Fusion if he got cut. Zuna is always two steps ahead of us."

"Maybe we're the ones who actually are *three* steps ahead of Zuna," Rock said. "Perhaps I anticipated that Zuna anticipated that I anticipated—"

"You're making my head hurt," Strike said. "Just get rid of him."

Pickaxe stepped forward. "I hate to admit it, but I think Rock might be onto something." He slugged Rock's shoulder. "You might hold the world record for dorkability. But you're brilliant. I love this idea."

"Dorkability?" Rock said. "What's dorkability?" He skimmed madly through his notebook as Pickaxe and Nugget broke into laughter.

Frak, Strike thought. *Why does Rock always have to be right?*

A thought popped into Strike's head. "Maybe you're right," he said. "I should at least talk to him."

"You should?" Rock asked. "Yes, you should." His eyes narrowed. "Why?"

Strike wished he could tell someone about his Ultrabot suit growing tighter by the week. But as trustworthy as his rocketback 2 was, Rock was terrible at keeping secrets. His poker face was nonexistent.

Which led to Fusion. Maybe the former Neutron knew what tech Zuna had used to enlarge Chain Reaction's Ultrabot suit.

Before Strike could speak, Fusion spewed out a mess of thoughts. "Look, I don't know what I'm doing here. I know this is a big surprise. I don't like surprises. They always turn out bad."

Strike froze. Then he laughed, a little of the tension melting away. "Totally. What I like is predictable. Reliable." He smacked Rock's shoulder. "I asked him to think outside the box, but I thought he'd come up with variations on zone defenses or something. Not bring in one of the greatest Ultraball players in history."

Fusion blushed, the corners of his mouth pulling into a tiny grin. "I'm not nearly as good as you. I depended on Chain Reaction to make the big plays." His smile vanished. "I'll never, ever get used to talking about Ultra-ball in the past tense. Sometimes I hit myself in the head, hoping I'll wake up from this frakkin' nightmare."

The wisp of a boy sniffled, and Strike felt his pain. Ultraball had been Fusion's entire reason for existing. On the field, Fusion had been a warrior, a hero, a mech beast, controlling one of the most powerful pieces of weaponry in the history of humanity. Nothing could replicate that feeling.

That feeling, which would soon be ripped away from Strike, too.

"Why did Zuna cut you and Chain Reaction?" Strike asked. "Did Chain Reaction outgrow his suit?"

"I don't know," Fusion said. "I haven't seen him since last year's Ultrabowl."

All the Miners looked at each other in confusion. The Fireball Five were together every day. Strike, Rock, and TNT met up with Pickaxe and Nugget without fail. It was crazy to think about not seeing one of them for months.

"It's not like we were that close," Fusion said. "I mean, except on the field."

Strike grabbed Fusion's shoulder. "Come with me. We have to talk."

"Where are you taking him?" Rock said.

"Just give me a moment with him, alone," Strike said. He motioned for Fusion to follow him.

Fusion trailed behind Strike toward the stands. The two of them went through a gate and climbed all the way up to the top row of seats.

Strike sat down, pointing to the seat next to him. He stared out into the giant cavern that had been his home away from home for four years, fixating on the words scraped into the opposite wall in ten-meter-tall letters:

MINERS TOGETHER, MINERS FOREVER

"You guys have the best home crowd in the game," Fusion said.

"Us?" Strike said. "You guys have the fiercest, most rabid fans ever. It's a nightmare playing in Neutron Stadium."

"Yeah. I hate Neutron fans."

Strike stared at Fusion, wondering if he was joking around. "What do you mean?"

"It's so uncool to throw trash and rocks at opposing teams. I was always so embarrassed."

"Why didn't you ever do anything about it?"

"Like what? Mr. Zuna controls everything. He would fly off the handle if I even paused before doing whatever he ordered me to. Sometimes I wonder if he knew that I didn't like the way he was doing things." Fusion paused. "I think that's why he cut me. What else could it be?"

"Were you outgrowing your suit?"

"Not even close."

"Hey," Strike said, trying to sound casual. "Is it possible that Zuna has a way of opening up an Ultrabot suit? I heard a rumor that Chain Reaction started outgrowing his suit two years ago, and that Zuna adjusted it so that he could extend his playing career."

"Modify an Ultrabot suit?" Fusion stared off into the distance. "Mr. Zuna is powerful. But no one on the moon understands Ultrabot suits enough to do something like that." He furrowed his brow. "Unless . . ."

Strike held his breath, that last word the key to his future. He waited, finally blurting out, "Unless what?"

Fusion shrugged. "I guess it's possible. Mr. Zuna does whatever it takes to win Ultrabowls. Chain Reaction was the key to our team, so Mr. Zuna would have gone to any length to extend his playing career. He has all sorts of incredible tech. I even heard he's somehow been stealing other teams' signals this year."

Strike nodded. This was exactly what he had been hoping to hear. If Zuna could find a way to enlarge an Ultrabot suit, then Strike could, too. Whatever it took, he had to extend his playing career so he could lead the Miners to their title. Fusion could be the key to that. But could Strike really trust a former Neutron?

"So you just followed two random Dark Siders who

popped up at your door?" Strike said. "No questions asked?"

"Lots of questions, of course," Fusion said. "But they told me that Boom sent them. That you could use my help, maybe even on the field. That sure got my attention." He leaned in. "Is she really still alive?"

Strike hesitated, wondering again if Zuna had put Fusion up to this. But there was no way Fusion could have gotten access to Dark Sider tunnels without Boom's help. The secret scoreboard message really was her way of helping the Miners finally win their title. "You have four Ultrabowl rings," he said, sidestepping Fusion's question. "How many other teams have come knocking at your door?"

"Zero. That would make Mr. Zuna so frakkin' mad."

"So you decided to come here and get Zuna pissed off at us?" Strike said.

"Oh, no, no, no," Fusion said, his eyes wide with horror. "Not at all."

"But there's a risk that Zuna will find out. Then you'd be screwed even worse than us. So why did you come?"

Fusion chewed on his lip and then shrugged. "You're the greatest quarterback to ever play the game. When you get the opportunity to hang out with one of your heroes—maybe even help him—you have to take it."

One of his heroes? Strike thought. *Is he talking about me?*

Fusion was the one with four Ultrabowl championships under his belt, not Strike.

They sat in silence, bashfully smiling at each other. Finally, Fusion said, "Look, I get why Rock invited me here. On paper, putting me in makes a ton of sense. But there's no way I could ever play Ultraball again. Mr. Zuna would murder me."

"I know that feeling," Strike muttered. "Kamar station."

"You think he was behind the attack?"

"Pretty sure of it."

Fusion nodded, turning back to the others. "Mr. Zuna doesn't mess around. You sure were lucky Nitro was there to sub in. She's incredible." He watched as Nitro, Pickaxe, and Nugget began a set of sprints, Nitro smoking the brothers. "Even if I could somehow play again, I think you ought to stick to Nitro. With time, I bet she'll become even better than TNT."

"Really?"

Fusion nodded. "In a lot of ways, she reminds me of Boom. And Torch. That one comet streak option, she threw a perfect pass to Rock. Her arm is incredible." He paused. "No offense to Rock or TNT. But you have a serious weapon. Use her."

"Huh," Strike said. "You really think so?"

"Yeah," Fusion said. "And don't forget who you're

playing this week—Torch's old team. Talk about motivation. Play up the fact that Nitro has a chance to get revenge on the team who blamed so much, so unfairly, on her brother. The Flamethrowers ruined both of their lives." Fusion stood up and headed toward the stairs. "I should go. I'm eating away at your practice time. Good luck against the Flamethrowers. Nitro will shred Afterburner if you turn her loose."

"Wait," Strike said. "Stay. I could use an extra pair of eyes. Especially when they belong to one of the best Ultraball quarterbacks in league history."

Fusion slowed and then stopped. He took a sidelong glance at Strike. "You mean that?"

"I do," Strike said. "If you're okay taking the risk of sneaking in and out of Taiko Arena for our practices, it'd be awesome to have you on our side." He hesitated. "You probably keep in touch with other Neutrons, yeah?"

"A little. Why?"

"You think . . ." Strike took a deep breath, holding it for a long time before letting it out. "Zuna is up to something big. You think you could dig up anything about what he's doing?"

Fusion's face melted into raw fear. His eyes bugged clear out of his head.

Strike swore at himself for going too far. "Never mind," he said. "Way too much to ask. Sorry."

But after a long pause, Fusion solemnly nodded. "I'll

never get over being cut so suddenly," he said. "After everything I've done for the Neutrons, Mr. Zuna at least owed me an explanation. So I'm going to find out why. And if I help out his archrivals in the process, that's just a bonus."

Fusion clenched his jaw, grinding his teeth. "Let's get you guys prepared for the Flamethrowers."

LOOSE CANNONS

Twenty seconds left before halftime. The Miners were up, but only 21–14 against a team that they should have been steamrolling. As he walked into the huddle, deep in their own territory, Strike glanced at the scoreboard to check the other games. The Neutrons had already won their matchup today, running up ninety-one points against the Yangju Venom. The Miners not only had to win this game to keep up with their rivals in wins and losses, but they had to score a whole lot more touchdowns to keep up in total points scored over the season.

Gotta keep my head in the game, Strike thought, knocking his gloved hands against his helmet. With a wince, he immediately regretted it, his shoulders twinging. If he was careful, he could keep the panic and pain under control and still play at his usual level. He couldn't afford to be stupid.

"Strike," Rock said. He motioned to the scoreboard. "Look. The dots and dashes at the bottom."

Strike swiveled around. "Another message. From Boom?"

"Yes, it has to be," Rock said. "Let's see. Dash dot—"

"The play clock is running," Strike said. He pointed at the head ref, who was signaling for play to begin. "Later, Rock."

"But what if this is an urgent message about what the Flamethrowers are doing right now?" He stared at the board, squinting. "I can do this in my head. It starts like the other one, dash dot dot dot—"

"Later!" Strike whacked Rock's chest plate hard enough to knock him back a step. "Focus. And don't stare straight at the scoreboard. Someone's going to notice."

"Oh yeah." Rock slapped his helmet. "Sorry."

"I don't want a repeat of last week," Strike said. "Promise?"

Rock nodded. But he stole another glance at the scoreboard.

With the play clock ticking down, Strike didn't have time to punch Rock again. After studying the Flamethrowers' defense, he touched the weapon strapped to his left arm. The arm cannons were Farajah Arena's new field feature this year, magnetic rail guns able to shoot the Ultraball at record speeds. The Flamethrowers, with all their home field practice, had learned to use them effectively. The other teams in the league had not. But needing a long pass here, and not trusting his ability to throw deep with any accuracy, Strike was going to fire the Ultraball and hope for the best. "Blast fly deadbolt forty-three!" he yelled. "Blast fly deadbolt forty-three!"

Poised over the ball in a three-point stance, Nugget swiveled backward to look at Strike. He flipped his helmet visor to clear, and his eyebrows went up.

"Do it," Strike said over helmet comm, his visor still set to reflective. "Turn around and do it."

Nugget did as he was told, but the look of concern never left his face.

"Hut," Strike barked. "Hut!" The ball came smacking into his hands, and he backpedaled quickly, loading the Ultraball into his arm cannon. He swiveled away from an oncoming defender, planted his feet, and charged forward. Raising his arm toward Rock, who was streaking up the middle of the field, he pulled the trigger.

Strike lurched backward, the weapon's recoil throwing him off his feet toward his own end zone. At the same time, the ball exploded out of the arm cannon, nothing but a silver blur.

A Flamethrower stuck an arm up, trying to block the pass. He got the fingertips of his glove on it, but it hit him with such force that it whipped his arm back, throwing him into an uncontrollable head-over-heels spin.

Rock's defender kept tight to him as they raced downfield, barely a step behind. The pass streaked in like a meteor, and the defender leapt at the same time as Rock. The Ultraball slammed into them with such power that it blasted both of them into a wild cyclone, their limbs flailing like they were rag dolls. The ball ricocheted off Rock's shoulder, straight upward, flying high.

Out of nowhere, Nitro came soaring in toward the Ultraball with a defender hot on her heels. She roared as she stretched to full extension, her back arched, outleaping her defender by mere centimeters. The ball clanged into her glove electromagnets.

As she fell to the turf, the defender lashed out with a roundhouse kick. The Ultraball knocked loose. All throughout the stadium, a frenzied cry went up: "Fumble!" The ball took a wild bounce, and another Flamethrower dove on it. He got to his feet and high-stepped past a diving tackle, and looked like he was off to the races. But Nitro somehow chased him down, launching herself at his legs, tripping him up. More Miners piled on to smash the Flamethrower to the ground. A buzzer sounded, signaling halftime.

The scrum slowly detangled, and Strike reached in to give Nitro a hand up. The crowd, mostly in the yellow jumpsuits of Farajah Colony, jeered and booed, chanting

Nitro's name in two long, derisive syllables.

"I'm so sorry I fumbled," she said. "I'm so stupid. That should have been a touchdown for us. I'm cursed. Just like my brother."

"No such thing as a curse," Strike said. "You had an amazing grab off the deflection. And your tackle at the end saved the touchdown going back the other way. Just try to hold on to the ball, okay? Turnovers will kill us."

"We're lucky you got into position after I couldn't reel in that pass," Rock said. He shook his head. "I can barely keep the Ultraball targeted on my sensors when it's traveling that fast, much less catch it."

Pickaxe got right up in Strike's face. "What the frak are we doing? The arm cannon is awesome, but it's too hard to control. Why aren't you just tossing up long bombs to Rock?"

Strike kept his helmet visor set to reflective. "Without TNT in the lineup, long bombs are too risky." He looked over to TNT, sitting glumly up in the Miners' coach's box.

"Yeah, but—"

"We're wasting time," Strike said, waving his teammates off the field.

"I hope we're going to make some adjustments," Rock said, jogging to try to catch up with Strike. "Big ones. The game is not going well."

The Miners headed back toward their locker room. They still had the lead, but the Flamethrowers had momentum and a big home field advantage on their side. Strike kept his eyes trained forward, struggling to come up with a solution. He thought back to Fusion's suggestion. Without any other ideas, it was their best shot at turning things around.

Strike unlatched the arm cannon from his left arm and hurled it toward an impactanium barrier, the weapon crashing into the wall with a metallic crack. He might have broken it, but he didn't care. "We're going to shake things up," he said over helmet comm. He slapped Nitro on the back. "We're turning her loose for the second half."

Nitro stopped suddenly. She flipped her visor to clear, her wide eyes full of worry. "Are you sure?" she asked. "Practicing all those plays with me as the feature rocketback is one thing. Using them in a real game? Against my brother's old team?" She lowered her voice. "The Torch's Curse was real, Strike."

"You're not cursed, and you'll be great," Strike said. "Let's get into the locker room. We need to lay out the new plan. We're going to run the entire offense through Nitro. This is your chance to make the Flamethrowers pay. Don't you want to get back at everyone who destroyed your and Torch's lives?"

"Of course I do. But do you really think I can do this?"

"Yeah. You're going to burn them, bad." Strike gave her a confident smile, trying to disguise how badly his insides were churning. Nitro was untested. Raw. And she was playing against a team whose fans had been booing her mercilessly, with signs all over the stands reading "THE CURSE, PART II."

But the Miners had no other choice.

Strike wasn't sure his halftime pep talk would do anything, but right from the second half kickoff return, Nitro played like a girl on fire. She was electric. Instead of waiting for the steel ball to arc down, she raced into a full sprint and catapulted off Rock's back, hurtling high to snatch the ball right out of the air. Nugget followed a second afterward, but took a lower trajectory to block for her.

Nitro and Nugget timed everything perfectly. Nugget smashed into the first defender, knocking the guy out of the play. Still in midair, he reached out to grab Nitro's hand. With a giant heave, he whipped her toward the end zone. The astonished Flamethrower defenders struggled to follow in pursuit.

Nitro landed twenty meters in front of the end zone and took off running. The closest defender made a desperate dive to stop her, swatting her ankle to send her into a roll. But she somehow popped to her feet and stumbled toward the goal line.

Two other defenders raced to stop her. She juked and faked. One of them locked a magnetized glove onto her shoulder plate and yanked her down. But Nitro twisted and sent a vicious kick at the defender's chest, blasting him away.

The other defender threw a chokehold around her neck. She lurched forward and threw him over her head, tossing him into the impactanium barrier separating the field from the stands. She waltzed into the end zone and spiked the ball. As it rebounded high off the turf, she jumped up after it and booted it midair toward the ceiling of Farajah Stadium. The ball shot up and cracked into the roof with a metallic ping. Nitro caught the ball as it ricocheted back. She held it victoriously over her head as she fell back to the field.

The pockets of Miners fans in the crowd went insane, people in blue jumpsuits on their feet, high-fiving each other, screaming for Nitro. A chant went up, repeating her name over and over and over. Meanwhile, the Farajah fans in yellow were stunned into silence.

No such thing as a curse, Strike thought. *Fusion is a frakkin' genius.*

After a four-and-out stop on defense, the Miners continued to roll on their next possession, capping off the drive with a surprise option pass from Nitro to a streaking Rock, her seventy-five-meter pass lasered in with perfect precision. It was a stunner of a throw—hardly any quarterbacks had such pinpoint accuracy on their long bombs, much less any rocketbacks.

As exciting as Nitro's astounding display of skill had been, it triggered a melancholy sense of loss in Strike. He used to be one of the few quarterbacks who could thread a full-field needle like that.

But then things started to go wrong. For every two highlight reel plays Nitro made, she cost the Miners with a fumble. Slowly, the Miners lost their lead and then fell behind. They tried to claw their way back, but they kept on losing momentum every time someone knocked the ball out of Nitro's hands.

Even after Strike spent the team's lone time-out in order to emphasize the importance of ball control, Nitro's fumbling problems continued. One fumble was understandable. Two was bad. Three was unforgivable. And four, in a single game? Now with just a minute to go, Strike's stomach churned, trying his best not to let the stress and pressure drown him. The Miners had just scored. But the Flamethrowers were up by seven, and they would be receiving the kickoff with very little time left.

It would take a miracle to pull out a win here.

The Miners would be kicking a dead drop—a desperation play that rarely resulted in recovering the ball—but Strike had managed a couple of successful dead drops over the years. He yelled out words of encouragement to his players. "We got this, guys. Nitro's on lead. She'll get it."

Nitro flipped her visor to clear. Her lips were pinched tight and trembling as she tried to keep it together under the immense pressure, but it looked like she might crack at any moment.

The Miners set up for the kickoff. They all charged ahead, accelerating across the line of scrimmage as Strike booted the ball high. With the huge amount of backspin he'd put on the ball, it arced sharply up toward the roof, hung for a long moment, and then plummeted like a rock, straight down toward the fifty-meter line.

As it dropped, a mass of players from both teams soared up in a clanging mass of yellow and blue Ultrabot suits, fighting and kicking for position. Afterburner, the Flamethrowers' rocketback 1, clawed his way up the mid-air scrum, kicking off his rocketback 2's helmet, leaping high to edge out Rock for the ball. It locked into Afterburner's electromagnetic gloves.

But as the mass of players fell back to the turf, Nitro shot in, slamming a devastating punch into Afterburner. The Ultraball popped out of his hands. Everyone snatched at it as it bounced crazily through people's grasps.

The Ultraball hit the turf, and Nitro dove for it. She scooped it up after just one bounce and barely broke stride as she took off. Two Flamethrowers stood between her and a game-tying touchdown.

"Do the smart thing!" Strike yelled over helmet comm. Going down safely and letting yourself get smothered would give the Miners the chance to strategize, to call a killer play that would tie up the score, with only thirty meters to go.

Nitro slowed, sliding to the ground, taking the safe route. Afterburner and Firestorm sprinted at her, ready to start a pileup. But as they jumped in to spear her, she rolled away and popped back to her feet, racing toward the end zone. She gave the last defender, Supernova, a hard jab-step and then spun around in an attempt to cut back the other way.

The Flamethrowers' quarterback bit on the fake, but he recovered quickly, racing at her, catching up. Nitro turned up the speed. She leapt for the goal line, stretching out her gloved hand, ready to slam the Ultraball down into the end zone for the touchdown. A split second later, a blur of silver came thwacking into Nitro: Supernova's arm cannon, which he had swung with all his might. It landed with a devastating crack, sending Nitro flying off her feet. She crashed to the turf, the Ultraball popping out of her glove.

Another player in Flamethrower yellow flew in, soaring through the air to pounce on the ball. Nugget slammed into him, the two of them careening toward the goal line. They wrestled to the turf, fighting and kicking. Everyone jumped on top of the scrum, throwing punches as they tried to worm their way to the bottom of the pile. Supernova picked up his arm cannon and swung wildly at anyone in blue. The mass of writhing impactanium Ultra-bots shoved backward and forward, momentum shifting every second, until everyone collapsed near the end zone as time ran out.

Fans in the stands held their breath as the refs rushed in to figure out what had happened. What with every player still trying to kick and punch out the Ultraball, it took the refs a full two minutes to disentangle the mass of flailing limbs.

The refs huddled together. Finally, the head ref stood up, facing the crowd. He pointed away from the end zone and blew his whistle.

The Flamethrowers had recovered Nitro's fumble. The game was over.

Strike collapsed to his knees. He banged his helmet into the turf, moaning in agony.

THE CURSE, PART II

By Aziz Chang, Grand Executive Reporter

In a true embarrassment, the Miners lost to the Farajah Flamethrowers this Sunday, 56–49, muffing what should have been an easy romp. Coming into the game, the Farajah Flamethrowers were in fifth place, their only prior win against the pitiful Saladin Shock in week one. But the Flamethrowers more than held their own against the hapless Miners, pulling off a huge upset.

The Miners were in a state of disarray all game long, the Flamethrowers taking full advantage of their team's arm cannon to blast the Miners in the face. The Miners could not respond.

The second half brought the unleashing of the Miners' new rocketback 1, Nitro, to astronomically negative results. While she did score five touchdowns, she also fumbled five times. Just like her brother, Torch—the quarterback whose last-second blunder cost the Flamethrowers the Ultrabowl VI title—Nitro also appears to be cursed.

The Miners' day was filled with problems. Strike underthrew Nitro three times, and got stopped twice on quarterback sneaks he should have broken for touchdowns. Strike played like a timid rookie all game long, only using his arm cannon a handful of times before ditching it in the second half.

With a 2–2 record, the Miners are in danger of falling out of playoff contention. So many questions surround them: TNT's continuing injury, Nitro's serious fumble issues, and Strike's cowardly play at quarterback. Can such critical matters be addressed?

At the postgame press conference, Strike had no answers.

Governor Katana of Taiko Colony attended the press conference as well. He smiled, saying, "I'm sure our Miners will bounce back. They always do." But he left in a hurry, beating a hasty retreat when asked for details on how the crumbling Miners could possibly save their sinking ship.

In another upset, the Cryptomare Molemen also lost, falling to the Tranquility Beatdown, 56–49. Wraith played a shaky game, throwing her first interception of the season and going for her fewest total meters gained. It appears her being under official investigation in connection with the string of nuclear component thefts has affected her play.

When asked about yet more parts being stolen from North Pole Colony's high-security facilities— four separate robberies now, including a miniature reactor that could potentially power a nuclear weapon—Raiden Zuna commented, "We will get to the bottom of these heinous felonies. I will not rest until justice is served and the United Moon Colonies are made safe once again. The Dark Sider terrorists who stole these parts are guilty of treason and will be given the death penalty."

Meanwhile, the North Pole Neutrons handily trounced the Yangju Venom, 91–28. After their loss to the Miners in week two, the Neutrons have regrouped in a major way, driven by the iron will of the team's heroic owner, Raiden Zuna. The Neutrons and the Beatdown sit atop the leaderboard, both with three wins and one loss. But the Neutrons have a whopping lead in the season tie breaker, with a tremendous seventy more total points scored. They are pulling away as the dominant team of the league, ready to crush all others.

RESULTS, WEEK 4

Flamethrowers	**56**
Miners	49

Neutrons	**91**
Venom	28

Explorers	**56**
Shock	35

Beatdown	**56**
Molemen	49

STANDINGS, WEEK 4

	Wins	**Losses**	**Total Points**
Neutrons	3	1	371
Beatdown	3	1	301
Molemen	3	1	287
Miners	2	2	287
Flamethrowers	2	2	280
Explorers	2	2	252
Shock	1	3	210
Venom	0	4	140

ROSTER CONTROVERSY

Two DAYS LATER, the Miners practiced inside Taiko Arena, everyone whacking away at the ball curled tightly in Nitro's gloved hands. They had been going at this for thirty full minutes, Nitro doing everything she could to not lose the ball.

Strike was watching from inside the coach's box, with TNT and Fusion sitting on either side of him. His eyes went in and out of focus as he tried to concentrate. Ever since the loss to the Flamethrowers, he had felt like he was on the verge of total breakdown. The raw fury was intense. *LunarSports Reports* blasted Strike 24/7, but even the unbiased media outlets were going nuts. The *Smash-Mouth Radio Blitz* was almost as bad, Berzerkatron and the Mad Mongol demanding that Strike do something to fix the team or step down as coach. Some of the more rabid Miners fans had even started a petition to get Strike to go to Moon Dock station and launch himself out the airlock, into the black void of space. Only the twenty-one colony governors knew the code to operate Moon Dock airlock, but there was no doubt that Raiden Zuna would have been happy to oblige. Almost every analyst and color commentator across the moon questioned Strike's abilities as general manager.

The worst part was that Strike did, too.

Even after sleepless nights of talking things through with Rock and TNT, he still couldn't figure out if he should stick to Nitro, or if he should try to call up someone else off his backup list. Maybe even try to convince Fusion to suit up for the Miners. Nitro had incredible talent, but she couldn't hold on to the ball. The only person who had fumbled more times in a single game was Torch, years ago, in his first game as quarterback for the Farajah Flamethrowers. Strike couldn't help wondering if they really were both cursed.

Strike turned to TNT, eyeing his midsection. "You feeling any better today?"

TNT put a hand on the left side of his belly, wincing as he did. "I want to suit up so bad. But if anything, it seems like it's getting worse."

Strike wished they could send him back to the hospital

to get checked out. But Rock had already stretched the Miners' meager budget, making magic happen to pay for the first visit. There was no possible way they could afford another. "You know what they say," Strike said. "Things will get a lot worse before they don't. Wait. How does that one go?" He looked to the field, where Rock had snuck up on Nitro and was whacking away at the Ultraball.

"Even I know that one," TNT said. "But I never understood it. Why do things have to get worse before they get better? Why can't they just get better?"

Strike sat in silence, contemplating TNT's question. Finally, he broke into laughter.

"What's so funny?" TNT asked.

"I don't know," Strike said. "Just makes me realize how stupid I am. Not a lot of things I'll be able to do after my Ultraball career is over."

Fusion silently dropped his head, his lips trembling.

"Frak," Strike said. "I'm such a moron. I didn't mean to—"

"It's okay," Fusion said, even though it clearly wasn't.

"I owe you, big-time," Strike said. "Genius idea to cure Nitro of her fumbling."

A thin smile came to Fusion's face. "Thanks again for letting me help out. Almost makes me feel alive again." His shoulders sagged forward. "Almost."

Strike closed his eyes, thinking back to Zuna's offer to enlarge his Ultrabot suit, sorely tempted to go back and take the deal.

A sharp crack made him jerk his head back to the on-field action. Nitro shook off Pickaxe and then Nugget, all the while cradling the Ultraball with both hands. She juked as Pickaxe leapt for her, high-stepping over his out-stretched arms. Rock leapt out of a field pit and bashed into her, but she protected the Ultraball against her chest plate like it was a stash of fresh food.

Strike nodded. "Time," he said into his headset. "Nice work, Nitro."

"I did it," she yelled into the helmet comm. "I did it!" She held the ball over her head. "No one knocked it—"

Pickaxe launched a huge roundhouse punch at the Ultraball. With a clang, it flew out of her glove.

Her visor flipped to clear, she turned to Pickaxe, who was beaming at her. "Let's see," he said. "What should I have you call me this time?"

"But that's not fair," Nitro said. "The play was over. I thought that . . . that . . ."

"Hey, Fusion," Pickaxe said. "What was your rule?" He grinned at Nitro.

"She knows it," Fusion said. He shrugged apologetically, but he couldn't stop the corner of his mouth from pulling up.

Pickaxe held a gloved hand to his ear. "So then remind me, what's Fusion's rule?"

"Anytime I let the Ultraball get knocked out, I have to call the person who knocked it out anything he wants," Nitro mumbled.

"Even if it's not during a play," Pickaxe added. "Any time at all. From the first moment you suit up and grab an Ultraball, to the last second before you click out. Right?"

"Right," Nitro said.

"Don't you mean, 'Right, oh great majestic wonder whose farts smell like gold'?" Pickaxe cracked up as he flipped his helmet visor to clear.

"I'm not saying that," Nitro said. She turned to Strike. "Come on. Do I really have to say that? How can farts smell like gold, anyway?"

With a wry smile, Strike shrugged. "Gotta do it."

"I hate you all," Nitro grumbled. But she turned to Pickaxe. "Fine. Oh great majestic wonder whose farts smell like gold." She gave him an exaggerated bow.

"Now that's better," Pickaxe said. "But your majesty demands an even deeper bow. More like this." He bent from the waist, one hand in front and one in back in a ridiculous display. "And would it kill you to give me a little curtsy? Just one girly little curtsy is all I'm asking for." He daintily put a foot out.

Nitro glared as Pickaxe laughed and bowed even farther, his head all the way down to waist level. She quietly picked up the Ultraball and raised it high. With a great big smile on her face, she smashed the ball across the back of Pickaxe's helmet, knocking him face-first to the ground.

As Nugget burst into maniacal giggles, Pickaxe looked up from the turf, his cheeks flushed with embarrassment. "Hey, you can't do that," he said.

"That's what you get for calling me girly," Nitro said. "And last time I checked, there was no rule about punishing frakkin' idiots for being total frakkin' morons on the field."

"She has a point," Fusion said.

Pickaxe opened his mouth to complain, but then he grinned. "Don't you mean, 'for being total morons, oh great majestic wonder whose farts smell like gold'?"

Nitro sighed, looking up to the coach's box. "How long are we going to do this for?"

"The entire season, all the way through the playoffs," Strike said. "It'll cure you of your fumbling." He called out to the others. "Okay, everyone. Back out to the end zone for more fumble drills."

As Nugget, Pickaxe, and Rock ran off, Nitro hung back for a moment. She turned to TNT, her eyes pleading. "You have to get better soon. So many people are talking about the Curse, Part II." She hung her head. "I can't take the pressure."

"I'll be back before you know it," TNT said. "By the playoffs for sure. Just hang in there, okay?"

Nitro took a deep breath and nodded. She cradled her Ultraball extra tight in both arms before trudging off toward the others.

As the Miners jogged toward the far end zone, Strike leaned in to whisper to Fusion. "Hey. Are you sure that—"

"Nitro is your best option at rocketback 1, bar none," Fusion said. "She even has a great arm. Her long bomb to Rock against the Flamethrowers was incredible. Right on the money. If someone asked me to start an Ultraball team with anybody I wanted, she would be at the very top of my list."

"Aside from me, right?" TNT said. He smiled, but there was a tinge of worry behind it.

"Uh. Right." Fusion turned away, staring at the Miners on the field.

"Don't worry," Strike said, nudging TNT. "No one is taking your roster spot. You saved my life back at Kamar station. I'll get you back on the field as soon as you're ready to go."

Holding his side, TNT took a pained breath and nodded.

Fusion pumped his fist as Nitro held on to the ball after a vicious triple-team attack from Pickaxe, Nugget, and Rock. "Carrying an Ultraball every moment she's suited up will force her to take care of it. Trust me. She's going to be a superstar. Look at how much everyone on the team loves her. If she could just find some confidence, she might even become league MVP. Take you guys all the way to a title."

Strike looked into Fusion's eyes. "If you were starting a team, you'd really take her over any other rocketback?"

"Without a shred of doubt," Fusion said. He stole a glance at TNT but quickly turned away. "She will lead you guys to the promised land. Just make sure she carries around that Ultraball any time she's suited up. Every practice, every game, every moment. From now, all the way through the Ultrabowl."

Strike took a hardtack bar out of his pocket and started gnawing on the nasty thing. As Rock had concluded, it was impossible to make the nutrient bars taste better. But as Strike watched Nitro juke out Rock with a fancy jab-step spin, all the time holding the Ultraball carefully tucked in, his confidence grew. *Maybe she can do the impossible. If I can just get her to believe in herself.* He swallowed, almost tricking himself into thinking that the bar tasted good.

Almost.

"Hey, Strike." Fusion paused. He glanced sidelong at TNT. "Can I talk to you? In private?"

"Anything you can tell me, you can tell TNT."

"Please." Fusion bit his lip. "It's kind of top secret."

Strike hesitated, but TNT shrugged. "It's cool." He got up and moved away, limping as he went.

After TNT got out of earshot, Fusion leaned in to whisper. "I met up with Radioactive in secret," he said. "Found out something."

"Yeah?"

"He heard that Mr. Zuna has developed ways of stealing other teams' signals. Really sneaky stuff. You gotta be extra careful."

"How is he doing it? Which signals?"

"Don't know. But there's more. A lot more." He huddled in. "Swear that you won't tell anyone you heard it from me? Mr. Zuna would cut my and Radioactive's throats if he ever found out."

Strike leaned over, crouching down. "I promise."

Looking over his shoulder to make sure no one was watching, Fusion leaned in. "Radioactive thinks Mr. Zuna ordered the attack at Kamar station."

"I knew it," Strike hissed. "He was aiming to take out TNT, wasn't he?"

"Radioactive doesn't know. Might have been you. But one thing is for sure: Mr. Zuna is hell-bent on winning the Ultrabowl. At any cost."

Strike blinked hard. He looked over to his injured rocketback sitting nearby—the boy who had taken a knife for him. "You trust Radioactive?"

Fusion nodded. "Ion Storm and the rest are Zuna's lackeys, but Radioactive is like a brother to me. He's scared. Mr. Zuna has done a lot of shady stuff in the past, but this is at a whole new level."

Strike sat quietly as he processed it all. Surprisingly, a thin smile came to his face. It was almost funny that Zuna's attack at Kamar station had resulted in Nitro stepping up. *How perfect would it be if she ended up leading us to an Ultrabowl victory over Zuna's Neutrons?* he thought.

"There's more," Fusion said. "I found out why Mr. Zuna cut me." He stopped, biting his lip. "Radioactive thinks that Mr. Zuna signed White Lightning because White Lightning was desperate. Desperate enough to be forced into doing a secret project. Late at night, Mr. Zuna has been working him to death. White Lightning has been suiting up. To build something big."

Strike's forehead wrinkled up. "That's illegal," he said.

"I know," Fusion said. "But I wouldn't put it past Mr. Zuna to send White Lightning sneaking around after dark, all suited up."

"Where's he going?"

"Don't know."

Strike sat back in thought. It was against league rules to use Ultrabot suits for anything except Ultraball. But it'd be relatively easy for someone to skulk around undetected during the moon's artificial night. Hardly anyone on the moon went out after dark. It'd be especially easy with an Ultrabot suit's high-tech sensors and lighting at your disposal. "What's he building?"

"Some sort of weapon."

Strike's heart stopped for a long moment. "What kind of a weapon? Like the Meltdown Gun?"

"He doesn't know," Fusion said.

"Then why does he think it's a weapon?"

Fusion's voice lowered to a hoarse whisper. "He heard a code name for whatever White Lightning is assembling." His lower lip trembled. "It's called Operation Deathstrike."

THE
SMASHMOUTH
RADIO BLITZ

BERZERKATRON: And we're back, the one-two punch of Berzerkatron and the Mad Mongol, breaking down the action around the league. The new-look Taiko Miners are today's hot-button topic, after crushing the Saladin Shock in week five, 98–63. I gotta admit, folks, I was dead wrong about Nitro. Yesterday, she put herself in MVP contention. With ten total scores—six receiving, three rushing, and one astounding full-field pass off the option, she almost broke the Miners' team record for touchdowns in a single game. She's so good, I think the Miners ought to stick with her, even when TNT is back from injury. No question about it—the Miners have the big mo: momentum. They might just go all the way.

THE MAD MONGOL: When you say "the big mo," you must mean "the big mo-ron." As in: you. The new-look Miners? Nitro had a great day, I'll grant you that. She looked almost as good as Chain Reaction in his prime. Whatever happened to that dude, anyway? But the Neutrons are still going to roll into the playoffs and then crush everyone.

BERZERKATRON: What, are you working for LunarSports Reports now? Zuna forcing you to pump up his Neutrons and talk smack about the Miners?

THE MAD MONGOL: Hey, now. It's all fun and games until someone gets accused of working for LunarSports Reports. Look. I give Nitro credit. She whupped on the Shock. Yanked down their Ultrabot suit trousers and turbo-spanked their bare bottoms. But it's just one game.

BERZERKATRON: Look at her leadership, though. The postgame press conference, where Nitro gave her teammates all the credit for the win?

THE MAD MONGOL: Okay, that made me laugh so hard I nearly pooped my jumpsuit. That question about her one fumble, recovered by Nugget—what was it that she called him?

BERZERKATRON: It sounded like "Lord Protector Whose Regal Butt I Must Wipe." That was frakkin' hilarious. And that's leadership, man. Raw, natural leadership. The team is already rallying behind her. They love her. You can see it in their eyes.

THE MAD MONGOL: All right, all right. But let's be real. No way they get past the Neutrons, who have all but guaranteed themselves the number one seed. As talented as Nitro is, she ain't never getting by Neutron Nation. Not at Neutron Stadium.

BERZERKATRON: Anything is possible in Ultraball. The Miners, the Beatdown, or the Molemen could all pull off an upset.

THE MAD MONGOL: *Dunno about that. The Mole-men are under a ton of pressure, their quarterback rumored to be connected to the North Pole Colony thefts. I thought that was more of the usual LunarSports Reports crap at first, but now I'm wondering if there's some truth to it. A slew of nuclear components mysteriously disappearing with no trace? And rumors of eerie footprints spotted down in the Tunnel Ring? Sounds like Dark Siders, all right.*

BERZERKATRON: *Criminal or not, all the scrutiny on Wraith had to have contributed to the Molemen's second loss in a row yesterday. After a hot start, they're struggling. Wraith has to find a way to turn her team around.*

THE MAD MONGOL: *Wraith. There's something bizarre about her. Showing up out of nowhere over the off-season, her and her teammates suddenly taking over an entire Ultraball roster? Some say it was genius, but I say it's creepy. The old ghost stories about someone— or something—haunting the Tunnel Ring after dark? Maybe it's been the Dark Siders all along. Is it any coincidence that one of the legends has a wraith as the one doing the haunting?*

BERZERKATRON: *Did you just admit that you believe in ghosts? And that Wraith is one? Who's the big mo-ron now? I really hope you ask her what it's like to haunt the Tunnel Ring. You'll get that chance to make a further fool of yourself tomorrow at the LunarSports QB Forum. For the first time ever, all eight Ultraball quarterbacks in the same studio, that's gonna be mega. Hard to believe that Strike finally agreed to do one of these things. Been four years since the Earthfart interview.*

THE MAD MONGOL: Anyone can slip up on the word "Earthfall" once. But five times? It's sad how he babbles and stammers under big-time studio lights. Hilarious, but sad. Yet another reason why the Miners will never win an Ultrabowl. When the pressure's truly on, Strike crumbles like a nasty ol' hardtack bar.

BERZERKATRON: Okay, wise guy. I'm putting my money where my mouth is. A hundred U-bucks on the Miners going all the way. They may not be the Fireball Five anymore. But now they're something even better. No TNT? No problem.

THE MAD MONGOL: You're on, Berzerkachump. Listeners, anyone else want a piece of this easy money? I'll take all bets from anyone dumb enough to say that the Miners have a chance in frakkin' hell. The phones are now open.

RESULTS AND STANDINGS, AFTER WEEK 5

RESULTS, WEEK 5

Miners	**98**
Shock	63

Flamethrowers	**91**
Venom	35

Beatdown	**91**
Explorers	84

Neutrons	**112**
Molemen	105

STANDINGS, WEEK 5

	Wins	Losses	Total Points
Neutrons	4	1	483
Beatdown	4	1	392
Molemen	3	2	392
Miners	3	2	385
Flamethrowers	3	2	371
Explorers	2	3	336
Shock	1	4	273
Venom	0	5	175

THE *LUNARSPORTS* QB FORUM

Two days after the Miners' win over the Shock, Strike led his team into one of the *LunarSports Reports* studios, a room full of audiovisual equipment beeping and whirring. It was a throwback to the pre-Earthfall era, a time when the brave moon colonists got anything they wanted. In this day and age, something as flashy as this studio was extremely rare. But now that Zuna owned *LunarSports Reports*, it was even more fully decked out, a modern-day technological palace.

Strike took a deep breath, trying to hold back the rising panic. Going on the *LunarSports Reports* QB Forum had seemed brilliant when Fusion had suggested it as a way to corner White Lightning and get him to spill his guts about Zuna's secret project. There was nothing Strike could do about the steadily increasing claustrophobia that might have affected his play against the Shock, perhaps even costing them a touchdown or two. But a much bigger contributor to his performance woes was the fact that something called Operation Deathstrike was hanging over his head.

At least, that's what he kept telling himself.

All the gleaming camera equipment and hordes of *LunarSports* reporters on Zuna's payroll made Strike's palms sweat. "Do we have to do this?" he asked Rock.

Rock squinted. "No, it's completely voluntary. You were the one who insisted on participating." He flipped open his notebook. "Just after our last game, in the locker room, you said—"

"Why do you have to be such a smart aleck?" Strike said.

"Smart aleck?" Rock said. "I was just repeating your words back to you."

"Exactly."

Standing behind them, Nitro cut in. "Strike also said that he was worried about freaking out on live TV because Raiden Zuna is going to be here. And because of all the *LunarSports* reporters blasting him about why we didn't blow out the Shock as much as we should have."

All the Miners turned to stare at her.

"What?" Nitro said, shrinking. "Did I get that wrong?"

Rock smiled. "No, you got it all perfect. I was thinking about saving up to buy you a notebook, but maybe you don't need one."

"What I need is for people not to remember all the dumb things I say," Strike muttered. Looking around the studio full of people who Zuna was paying to talk trash about him, he shuddered. He was terrible in interviews, especially in prime time ones like this. Ever since the infamous Earthfart interview four years ago, he'd sworn off these gigantic media shows. But this was important. He'd just have to find a way to survive the next grueling hour—and then figure out how to get White Lightning alone.

"We should scram," TNT said. "We're in Zuna's territory. It's not going to be pretty."

Strike slowly shook his head. "I have to know what Operation Deathstrike is."

"Most likely a ploy to keep you off balance," Rock said as he scribbled in his notebook. "It's very possible that Zuna ordered Radioactive to leak it to Fusion. We should leave."

"Easy for you to say. You'd think differently if White Lightning was working on a secret project called Operation DeathRock."

"He'd come up with something much more clever than that." Rock flipped pages, landing on one titled "Phrases with the Word 'Rock' in Them." "Ah! 'Operation Rock Crusher.' That would have been good."

"Good? Or terrible? Especially considering Zuna has already tried to have me killed?"

Rock's face fell. "You have a point. I suppose I'd want to find out anything I could, no matter how improbable it is that you'll be able to get White Lightning alone. Or that he's willing to talk. Or that he has any useful information. Or—"

"You're not helping," Strike said. "He'll talk if I can get him alone. He owes me, after I didn't force him to go one-on-one on the last play of our game. I have to find out about Operation Deathstrike."

And how to enlarge an Ultrabot suit, Strike thought.

TNT shook his head. "I wish you'd just focus on playing Ultraball. On winning the Ultrabowl. But if this will help get this stupid Operation Deathstrike monkey off your back . . ." He raised his eyebrows.

"Look, there's Destroyer," Nitro said, pointing to the quarterback for the Tranquility Beatdown. "He's so cute."

"Cute?" Pickaxe asked. He grumbled. "No one ever calls me cute."

"That's because your face looks like my butt," Nugget said.

"Okay, that's it. I'm gonna—"

"Cut it out, you two," Strike said. He craned his neck

around, but White Lightning was nowhere in sight. He caught a glimpse of Wraith, surrounded by her teammates. They locked eyes, and she raised her eyebrows at Strike. There was something in her look. Something urgent.

Strike took a step toward Wraith, but a *LunarSports* worker in a beige jumpsuit came over to intercept him. The corner of his mouth curled up into a wry grin. "There you are," he said in a smarmy voice. "This QB Forum is going to be spectacular. Ready to be grilled?"

Before Strike could sputter out a response, the main studio door opened to a wave of big guys in the red jumpsuits of North Pole Colony. White Lightning, tiny compared to his posse of grown men, shuffled in, looking more like a prisoner than the quarterback of the league-leading Neutrons.

Raiden Zuna walked in right behind his quarterback. His jeweled right hand glittered under the studio lights, his four Ultrabowl rings sparkling in brilliant starbursts. The entire mob in red headed toward Strike.

"Looking forward to seeing you up onstage, Strike," Zuna said, a grin smeared across his face. "No reason to be nervous. Only several thousand people hanging on your every word." He shot a glance toward a group of his reporters, who chuckled as they pulled out notebooks.

Strike choked back a glob of vomit climbing up his

throat. He looked to Rock with wild eyes, willing his friend to give him a good comeback.

Rock quickly caught on to Strike's look of desperation. He whipped open his own notebook, flipping through and landing on a page titled "Clever Comebacks." "Brilliant is as brilliant does," he said triumphantly.

Everyone stared at Rock until the boy's smile melted away.

Zuna raised an eyebrow at Strike. "That's really the best your sidekick could do?" he asked.

"He's not a sidekick," Strike said. "He's a genius."

"Genius is as genius does?" Rock said timidly.

Zuna and his entourage burst into laughter, a crowd of *LunarSports* reporters following suit. Before Strike knew what was happening, Zuna had put a hand on his back, ushering him toward a corner of the studio. "Let's go talk," he said. The bodyguards in red blocked off the rest of the Miners as Zuna pushed Strike through a side door and shut it behind them.

Inside the room, Zuna leaned into Strike. "Terrible games against the Flamethrowers and the Shock. Your gameplay is deteriorating so fast that I don't have to tell *LunarSports* to make up things anymore. Be smart for once. Give up Boom, and I'll extend your Ultraball career. This is your last chance."

"I told you, she's dead," Strike said.

Zuna's upper lip curled into a snarl. "Give me Boom or suffer the consequences. I won't let you stand in the way of justice."

Strike tried to stand his ground, to not shrink away from the man who had ordered an attack on the Miners just a few weeks ago. "You're bluffing," he said, his voice rising high.

"I don't need to bluff. Ask your buddy Fusion."

A surge of panic shot through Strike. His arms tensed, trembling. "What are you talking about?" he stammered. "Fusion isn't my friend."

"Don't insult me by denying that he's been sneaking into your practices." Zuna's lips pressed into a taut line. "You hear what happened this morning?"

Strike's breath caught in his chest. *No*, he thought. *This can't be happening.*

"Fusion was arrested," Zuna said. "Suspected in connection with the miniature nuclear reactor stolen out of North Pole Colony."

Strike's knees went wobbly, nearly buckling. Fusion was just a kid. He wasn't a criminal. *Zuna had Fusion arrested because he was helping me.*

"How did you find out?" Strike stammered.

"I have my ways," he said.

Something Fusion had said clawed its way into Strike's woozy head: *Zuna has developed ways of stealing other teams' signals. Really sneaky stuff.*

"Think very carefully about your future, Strike," Zuna said. "If you don't give me Boom, all the blood will be on your hands. For the safety of the UMC, I'll be forced to wipe the moon of all its filth."

Strike's paralysis turned to confusion as he looked into the demon eyes laser-locked on him. What did Zuna mean about wiping the moon of all its filth?

A knock sounded at the door. "Mr. Zuna, sir?" came a meek voice. "We need to start soon. Is that okay with you?"

Zuna put a finger up to his mouth, then drew it across his neck. He opened the door back into the main studio. "Can't wait to get this show on the road," he said casually. "Strike has all sorts of interesting things going through his head."

Strike slumped to the floor, struggling to hold it together as he raced through every one of Zuna's words, his facial expressions, his piercing looks. Whatever his threat had meant, it was certain that it wasn't just Strike's and Boom's lives on the line anymore. Zuna's words squeezed his head like a vise, crushing Strike a thousand times worse than his tightening Ultrabot suit.

Rock and TNT forced the door open with a bang. "Zuna's bodyguards kept us out," Rock said, breathing hard.

TNT jolted at the sight of Strike curled up on the floor. "You okay? What happened?"

Strike tried to speak, but he kept on choking on his words. Finally, he said, "I have to talk to White Lightning, alone. It's more important than ever."

TNT and Rock looked at each other, worried. But before they could ask for more details, several *LunarSports* people knocked and then banged on the door, forcing the Miners to get back out into the studio. Strike wanted to run away, but he had to talk to White Lightning. If he couldn't find a way to stop Operation Deathstrike, he'd have to give up Boom.

Inside the main studio, all the other quarterbacks had arrived. Even Governor Katana was there, standing against one wall, glancing sidelong at Zuna. He caught sight of Strike, and he made a beeline over, his pace urgent. But halfway there, he was blocked by a set of *LunarSports* reporters working to get everyone into place. Katana mouthed a word to Strike before the *LunarSports* people ushered him away:

Earthfall.

Strike inwardly groaned. As if he didn't have enough to worry about, now he had to figure out what Governor Katana was talking about. It was probably the fact that *LunarSports* was going to try to trick him into saying "Earthfart" again. But what if the governor was reminding him about Zuna being on par with the Earthfall Eight? Maybe Katana had even discovered something about

Operation Deathstrike and was trying to warn him about his impending doom.

When he saw the order of nameplates, Strike groaned again. He had been placed on one end of the long interview table, and White Lightning was all the way at the far end. How was he ever going to get to talk to White Lightning alone? Sweat was already beading on his forehead, and the heat of the spotlight was making things worse. Someone dabbed at his face with a towel. He stole anxious glances at White Lightning, who was being escorted up to the stage by two big bodyguards. Even with makeup caked on, he looked worse than Strike remembered, the dark folds of skin under his eyes nearly black now. His face was mottled with angry red spots.

One of the *LunarSports Reports* people in the back of the room waved his hand. "Places, everyone," he said. He fixed his gaze onto a giant clock hanging on the wall. "We'll be live in sixty seconds."

"Why are you staring so hard at White Lightning?" a voice whispered into Strike's ear, making him flinch.

Strike hadn't even noticed Wraith come up onstage, carefully sidling up to him. "I have to talk to him alone," he whispered.

Wraith started to say something, but the interviewer stepped onto the stage amid a buzz of activity. She closed her mouth and studied White Lightning, who had finally met Strike's eyes with surprise and alarm.

The interviewer, dressed in a crisp beige jumpsuit, smiled as he swept his gaze across the eight kids in front of him. But when he looked at Strike, there was malice in his grin. He turned to the main camera and flashed his brilliant white teeth. "This is Aziz Chang, grand executive reporter for *LunarSports Reports*. It's my pleasure to bring you an amazing special: all eight quarterbacks of the Underground Ultraball League, together in the same room for the first time ever. We'll go over the friendships, rivalries, and everything you ever wanted to know about the immense pressure that these eight Ultraball quarterbacks are under."

He turned his gaze onto Strike. "How is it that these kids, none older than age thirteen, don't fall apart under the crushing expectations and the tremendous implications of failure?" He moved in close to Strike, staring him down. "Speaking of that, we'll be spending a lot of time with Strike. We have so many questions about his thoughts on the silent but deadly forces that led to Earthfall."

Strike choked, erupting into a storm of coughing.

The interviewer's face lit up, full of glee. "We unfortunately have to take a very short commercial break before we launch in," he said. "But stay tuned for the panel session you've all been waiting for. As you can already tell, this is going to be sensational." As soon as the cameramen looked up from their posts, the interviewer openly chuckled at Strike.

Wraith hovered over Strike, who had doubled over, trying to catch his breath. Everyone stared, including Zuna, who motioned angrily to the *LunarSports* people to intervene. But as two workers moved in to separate them, Wraith leaned in close. "You okay?" she hissed into his ear.

Strike tried to say no, that all the pressure was making him freak out. But as he thought about getting out of his chair and running, he locked eyes with White Lightning at the far side of the table.

The boy was paralyzed with fear.

"I'll create a distraction," Wraith said. "Then it'll be up to you." Before she could say more, the *LunarSports* people swooped in, ushering her back to her seat. Someone pressed Strike back down into his chair as he tried to get his coughing under control.

The main interviewer came over, arching his eyebrows at Strike, a crooked grin on his face.

"Everyone, quiet," a *LunarSports Reports* cameraperson hissed. "We're back on, in three . . . two . . . one . . ." She pointed to the interviewer.

How the frak am I going to get White Lightning alone? Strike thought.

But his worries trailed away as Wraith got to her feet, a towering presence. Her eyes darted from Strike to

White Lightning and back again. Then she pounded both fists onto the table, spittle flying out of her mouth as she yelled at Strike. "You think I'm going to just stand here and do nothing? I heard what your teammates said about us."

Strike froze for a long moment before realizing what was happening. "We meant it," he said, pointing an accusing finger at her. "That thing I said." He paused. "You know what I'm talking about."

"Everyone calm down," the interviewer said. "Let's get back to . . ." He looked toward the studio director, who was madly waving a cue card that read "Keep It Going." He nodded and stepped out of the way.

"Calling me a second-rate hack who can't throw?" Wraith said. She took a step toward him, straightening her white jumpsuit. "That's one thing, because it's just dumb. We put the smackdown on you back in week one." She whipped around, narrowing her eyes at the rest of the Miners. "But what Pickaxe said is unforgivable. The Cryptomare Molemen aren't going to stand for that kind of talk from a loudmouthed moron." She motioned to her teammates, all four of them coming up to the stage.

Pickaxe put his hands up defensively and started to protest, but Nugget caught Strike's long glare. He jabbed his brother with a hard elbow to shut him up.

In spite of the tension, Strike grinned. Nugget was the youngest Miner, but he was often the most perceptive, especially when it came to understanding his coach's intentions.

"A lot of talk," Wraith said. "You gonna keep saying all that stuff now that me and my teammates are right here in person?" She pointed toward the Miners. "Why don't you get your flunkies up here, and we'll see how much you can really back up?"

Strike motioned his teammates up to the stage. "This is your chance, Pickaxe," he said. "Tell Wraith what you said about her mother. 'Yo mama's so dumb, she ate a hardtack bar and it tasted even worse than ever'?"

"I didn't say that," Pickaxe croaked as Nugget and the others dragged him up to the stage.

Rock flipped through his notebook. "It doesn't even make sense," he mumbled.

"You think I'm going to let you get away with that?" Wraith asked. She grabbed the front of Pickaxe's blue jumpsuit, pulling him forward, his eyes wide in terror. "The Molemen fight back." She spun around and threw Pickaxe clear across the room, sending him barreling into White Lightning. Both of them crashed to the floor.

"Fight!" one of the Molemen yelled. All the Molemen rushed the stage as Wraith jumped at Strike, her fists flying. Players from other teams stormed in to protect their team's quarterback. Soon, it turned into an all-out, bare-knuckle brawl.

In the middle of the chaos, Strike ducked to the

floor and crawled his way toward White Lightning. But not even halfway there, someone kicked Strike in the stomach. Searing pain exploded in his back as someone slammed him with a kidney punch. People piled up on top of him, squashing him flat.

Just as the edges of his vision started to fade, all the pressure on top of him was lifted. Pickaxe's face came into focus by his side. "Are you okay?" he asked.

Strike managed to nod as he took heaving breaths.

"Good, because I'm going to kill you," Pickaxe said. "Did you really have to use me as a distraction?"

"It was the only way," Strike wheezed.

Gradually, the melees around the room petered out. Teammates and *LunarSports* people pulled apart wrestling and punching matches between kids dressed in all different jumpsuit colors. Strike scanned the room, searching for White Lightning. But all the players in red jumpsuits were being shuttled away to safety by a posse of bodyguards. White Lightning was already gone.

Strike slapped his hands to his head. "We missed him. I messed it all up. Like I mess everything up."

"I don't know about that," TNT said. "I think we got what we came for."

"To get humiliated on national TV?" Strike said.

"Well, yeah. But the fight was the perfect distraction. Wraith, she's a genius." TNT looked around to make sure no one was listening in. "During the brawl, Big Bertha stayed close to White Lightning. She stepped in and took a punch to the gut—a punch that was aimed at him. I stayed with her and ended up getting slugged, too."

"Whoa," Pickaxe said in awe. "Did it hurt?"

TNT shrugged. "It wasn't that bad, but I played it up, big-time. I told White Lightning he owed me one. I also reminded him how you took it easy on him during our regular season game, not forcing him to go one-on-one like last year."

Strike leaned in, pumping a fist. "He talked. I knew he would."

"We didn't have much time before his bodyguards ripped him away." TNT looked nervously around the room. "You were right, Strike. Zuna is forcing White Lightning to build some kind of weapon, way more powerful than the Meltdown Gun. It's called the Deathstrike Device."

Strike's breathing went ragged. His vision blurry, Strike slumped into Rock, who struggled to keep him upright. There is was again—the word "Deathstrike." Zuna was going to murder him. And given what Zuna had said about wiping the moon of all its filth, Strike's murder would be just the start.

"He was on the verge of breaking down, saying that Zuna would eject him out of Moon Dock airlock into space if he ever found out he talked," TNT said. "But I pressed him anyway. Kept on telling him that he owed both you and me in a huge way. He finally said that we need to talk to Chain Reaction. Apparently, he knows everything about Operation Deathstrike. Every last detail."

"Where is he?"

"Salaam Hospital."

"He's sick?"

TNT nodded. "In intensive care. But he's not just a patient." He paused. "He's a prisoner."

Strike let out a tortured moan. Salaam Hospital was hard enough to get into. If Zuna had put in even more security measures, it would be impossible to get to Chain Reaction. "We're screwed," Strike said. "Everyone on the moon is so screwed."

Strike looked around to his Miners, hoping that one of them would have a brilliant plan. Surely, Rock would know what to do next. But all of them just stared at each other, no one saying a word. Strike grabbed at fistfuls of his hair, his world spiraling out of control. He had no choice. He had to give up Boom to Zuna.

"It's that important to talk to Chain Reaction?" came a quiet voice.

Strike looked up at Nitro, whose jaw was trembling.

"It is," Strike said. "Life and death. For a lot of people."

Nitro's gaze dropped to the ground, her jaw quivering even harder. She thought for a long time, her face twisted in agony, on the verge of tears. "Then I think I can get you into the hospital."

"Really?" Strike said. "How?"

"I know someone who works there." She let out a strangled breath. "My brother."

LunarSports *Reports around the League*

NEUTRONS THRASH EXPLORERS

By Aziz Chang, Grand High Executive Reporter

In a show of utter domination, the North Pole Neutrons set a new UUL record for points scored, crushing the Kamar Explorers, 126–49. The defending champion Neutrons look all but invincible. White Lightning threw for six touchdowns, and Meltdown scored eleven times, near a league record. The electrifying duo looks unstoppable, much more so than the old one-two punch of Fusion and Chain Reaction. With Fusion's recent arrest and imprisonment, the roster switch from Fusion to White Lightning once again points to Raiden Zuna's foresight and genius.

With the romp, the Neutrons have secured a spot in the playoffs. And with a whopping 147 more total points scored than their closest competitor, they are poised to lock up the number one seed.

Meanwhile, the Beatdown, once thought to be contenders for the Ultrabowl title, are officially a team in decline. They played woefully against the horrendous Saladin Shock, nearly getting upset by the second-worst team in the league. It was only a last-minute pick-seven interception by Uppercut that sealed the Beatdown's win, 70–56. At the postgame press conference, their quarterback, Destroyer, appeared to be shaken by the close shave. When asked why they played so badly, he said, "Hammer Fist wasn't feeling good right before the game. We would have pulled him, but there wasn't enough time to get someone off our backup list." Destroyer then continued to make weak excuses for his team's terrible play.

Meanwhile, the Miners shamelessly took advantage of the lowly Yangju Venom, running up the score on a hapless team, 119–28. Some so-called experts have argued that it was the Miners' duty to score as many points as possible since the tie-breaker is total points scored over the season. But only a cowardly bully embarrasses an opponent so badly.

The Miners' rocketback 1, Nitro, was a small bright spot for the Miners, scoring eight touchdowns, including a fingertip grab of one of the few long passes that Strike threw all game, this one badly off target. Some commentators have even mentioned her in MVP discussions. One huge question remains, though: What will the Miners do when TNT is recovered from his injury? He was again kept off the roster, making it four straight games now. But an anonymous source reported that TNT had been yelling at Strike that he had been ready to go, and that he should have been playing.

Strike skirted that roster issue during the post-game press conference, saying, "No comment. Mind your own frakkin' business." It was telling how defensively he reacted, appearing to have a major team chemistry problem brewing.

Week-seven action will determine the final playoff seedings, with the Beatdown, Miners, and Molemen jockeying for position in an attempt to stay out of the dreaded fourth seed. The best way to describe the overall playoff picture is through the current percentages set by the oddsmakers:

Team Chance of Winning the Ultrabowl

Neutrons 61 percent

Miners 15 percent

Molemen 13 percent

Beatdown 11 percent

RESULTS, WEEK 6

Miners	**119**
Venom	28

Beatdown	**70**
Shock	56

Molemen	**84**
Flamethrowers	56

Neutrons	**126**
Explorers	49

STANDINGS, WEEK 6

	Wins	Losses	Total Points
x-Neutrons	5	1	609
x-Beatdown	5	1	462
Miners	4	2	504
Molemen	4	2	476
Flamethrowers	3	3	427
Explorers	2	4	385
Shock	1	5	329
Venom	0	6	203

x = *clinched playoff spot*

FALLEN STAR

A DAY AFTER their romp over the Yangju Venom, Strike sat quietly in disguise as he rode a Tunnel Ring tram, his face and jumpsuit caked with dirt and filth. He stared out the window as the tram slowed and then did its obligatory stop at Moon Dock station. An eerie chill tingled up his spine as he squinted at the airlock door at the far end of the cavern. *Why did Rock have to notice how weird it was for the door to have no dust on it?* he thought. As if there weren't enough things for Strike to worry about. The last thing he needed to think about was the ghastly unending blackness of outer space beyond the door, and the dead planet Earth, nuked to oblivion by the tyrants known as the Earthfall Eight. It was slowly dawning on Strike that

Zuna might be even worse than those eight power-hungry dictators. He flinched when the tram beeped, its doors closing before it exited the station.

Trying not to think about the horrors of outer space made him think about them even more. Kids back at the Tao Children's Home told ghost stories about monsters from other planets, wraiths held at bay by the airlock door, waiting for their chance to cross the threshold to feed off people's nightmares. *Maybe the door has no dust on it because something's opened it*, Strike thought.

He jolted in alarm when he spotted what looked like a set of footprints inside the Tunnel Ring, near the wall. Throwing himself up against the window, he strained to focus on what he had seen, but the tram had already moved out of range.

Shivers wracked his entire body, the terror mounting. This was Operation Deathstrike. In just a matter of seconds, he was going to die.

Squeezing his eyes tight, he struggled to fight back his panic. He managed to eke out a small chuckle. All the rumors about something haunting the Tunnel Ring late at night were stupid. There were no such things as monsters. Or ghosts. Ghosts didn't leave footprints, anyway. Or use doors, for that matter. And he couldn't have seen footsteps, because the tram had been moving too fast. He was being ridiculous.

Wasn't he?

A beep sounded as the tram slowed, approaching Salaam Colony's station. Strike let out a sigh of relief at the opportunity to think about something else besides ghosts. His heart sped up, thumping in his chest as he scanned for Torch. Images from years ago flashed through Strike's head, of the superstar in bright Flamethrower yellow, Farajah Colony fans screaming at the tops of their lungs for the savior who was going to take their team back to the Ultrabowl. Torch had been on fire. He had been one of the best players in the history of the game, but more importantly, one of the greatest minds.

Strike spotted a hunched-over teenager who looked a little like Torch, except that this guy was way older, with a wrinkly gray face and heavy folds of skin sagging under his eyes. Strike continued to scan the tram station, but he couldn't find Torch anywhere. *Where is he?* Strike thought, increasingly worried. Nitro had said that her brother would meet Strike at the station and go over the plan to sneak inside the hospital.

Strike wandered through the crowds, searching for Torch. As the moments passed, Strike got more and more paranoid, wondering who might see through his disguise. Dressed in a pink jumpsuit of a Guoming Colony junker, he'd be pretty much ignored wherever he went on the moon. He kept on glancing at the Blackguards by the airlock door. All it would take was for one of them to recognize him, and then there would be trouble. If Zuna could have Fusion arrested and hauled into Han-Shu Prison, he could do the same for Strike.

"Nice disguise," someone whispered into his ear.

Strike jolted. It was the old guy who looked a little like Torch. But as Strike studied the guy's face, a horrifying realization struck him. "Torch?" he said. "You look terrible. I mean . . ." He winced at his ever-present stupidity.

Torch gave him a melancholy smile. "The disguise didn't take much. It's been a rough couple of months."

"Nitro—er, Jasmine—says you've been working here?"

"Among other places," Torch said. "I pick up work wherever I can. Another two years and I'll have paid off her medical bills."

Strike's eyes widened. "How much do you owe?" he asked.

"Not easy to earn five thousand U-bucks." Torch looked away. "Well, forty-five hundred. I did make some money selling . . ." He gulped. Although Torch towered over Strike, he looked like a little kid melting in shame, his head hung low in front of a disappointed parent.

"Let's not talk about that," Strike said. "Can you really get me in to see Chain Reaction?"

"I think so," Torch said. "It's not going to be easy. But I'm pretty sure you'll have maybe five minutes with him before the guards come."

"Five minutes? That's it?"

"The security around Chain Reaction's room is super tight. I'm not even sure it'll be five minutes."

Strike studied the Blackguards at the front of the line, checking IDs. "So how are we going to do this?"

"First, we have to get you past those guys," Torch said. "Here." He handed Strike an ID badge.

"Where did you get this?" Strike asked. A stupid grin stretched across his face as he read the name on the front. "Riku Kawasaki. Wildfire's real name."

"I thought you might get a kick out of that," Torch said. "No one remembers Wildfire anymore." The corner of his mouth crinkled. "No one ever remembers the losers."

Strike slowly nodded. It wasn't fair that Wildfire— Torch's old crackback 2—had faded from everyone's memory. Despite having lost the Ultrabowl, they had made it to the big game, against all odds. That entire Flamethrowers squad deserved a place in history. Strike turned away as memories of last year flooded through his head, of him and Torch talking Ultraball like old buddies.

Torch kicked at some pebbles on the station floor. "I'm going to make up for last year, I swear it. I'll get you in. It's going to take a lot of coordination. And some luck." He glanced over his shoulder and held out his hand, a folded piece of paper hidden in his palm. "Here's the plan."

Strike took it as nonchalantly as he could, covering it with his other hand to protect it from prying eyes. As he studied the details and diagrams, his breath caught. "Will this work? It can't. Can it?"

"I've been over it a hundred times. I know all the security protocols now." Torch nodded. "It took me a ton of time. And money. But I'm sure it can work."

"You had to spend money to make this happen?" Strike asked.

"Fake ID badges don't come for free," Torch said. "But don't worry about it. I have a debt to you that I can never fully pay off. Even if you never forgive me, at least I'll die knowing that I spent the rest of my life trying to make things right."

As if Strike hadn't felt conflicted enough, he felt even worse now. Torch had spent money on this crazy mission of Strike's—money that Torch badly needed, to continue paying off Nitro's hospital bills. "Nitro is lucky to have you as a brother," Strike said.

Torch peered out of the corner of his eye at Strike. "How is she? Been a long time since I've seen her. Not since . . . you know."

Strike looked over in surprise. "You haven't seen her since last year? How did she arrange this, then?"

"Through a mutual friend. She doesn't want to talk to me ever again." Torch sighed. "She has this crazy idea that I should have let her die. Better than saddling her with all the guilt that she carries around with her now. But you know what?" He thrust his jaw out, his eyes steely. "I'd do it all over again. Ever since our parents died, she's all I have left. The most important thing is that she's still alive. That's all that matters."

Strike wanted to keep hating Torch for selling out the Miners. But a similar thing had happened with TNT two years ago, when he had sold out to Raiden Zuna in order to protect his mom's safety. Strike had learned to forgive TNT, wanting so badly to help his best friend gain redemption.

Shouldn't I forgive Torch, too? he thought.

Maybe he and Nitro both should.

"Keep your head down so they don't notice anything," Torch said. "Junkers always look down at the ground." He nudged Strike's hand. "And eat that piece of paper. Talk about collecting garbage and cleaning up and stuff."

The two of them mumbled to each other about their long days ahead, Strike doing his best to pretend he was an actual junker from Guoming Colony. Even when he had been an orphan at the Tao Children's Home, he'd been higher on the social ladder than junkers. He had to admit, Torch had come up with a really good plan.

When they got to the front of the line, Torch handed his ID badge to one of the guards, his eyes fixed onto the ground in a submissive pose. "Taj Tariq, sir," he said.

"Okay, Tariq," the guy said. "Next."

Strike handed the Blackguard his fake ID badge,

forcing himself to stare at a spot between his feet. Waves of heat rose from his head as he waited for the guard to let him through. But seconds passed, and nothing happened. Strike didn't dare look up for fear that the guy would recognize him. A trickle of sweat ran down Strike's back.

The guard took out his billy club and jabbed Strike. "Are you mute, or just a moron? State your name."

"My name?" In a flash of panic, Strike realized that he had forgotten what was on his ID badge. It was the real name of a former Ultraball star. But which one? It was someone that both he and Torch admired, an underrated player.

"Do we have a problem, you dirty frakkin' junker?" the Blackguard said. "State your name."

"Uh." Strike tried to swallow, but his throat was raw. "I. Uh. What?"

"Stupid frakkin' idiot," Torch said. He grabbed Strike by the front of his jumpsuit and threw him hard to the ground. "Can't even remember his name. Riku Kawasaki, dumb as a bag of rocks." He jabbed a kick to Strike's ribs before shooting a quick glance to the guards. "Stupid frakkin' frakhead."

The Blackguard nodded. He leaned over and spit in Strike's face. "Get up." He dropped the fake ID onto Strike's head. "I said, get up." Raising his billy club, he readied to blast Strike with it.

Torch quickly scooped up Strike, who was moaning

and clutching his ribs, and ushered him in. The airlock doors slid open when a guard pressed the entry button, and they slid closed behind them.

Strike was still doubled over, trying to catch his breath. Torch propped him up, keeping both of them walking forward. "I'm so sorry about that, Strike," Torch whispered. "I had to do something. Violence is sometimes all the Blackguards can understand."

Strike tried to say that it was okay, but he couldn't speak through the pain. All he could think was if this was the easy part of the plan, the hard part might end up with him and Torch dead.

INS AND OUTS

INSIDE HIS COFFIN-LIKE space, Strike struggled to keep the claustrophobia at bay. He kept breathing slowly and deeply like Torch had told him to. Each breath of the dank air felt as if it contained less and less oxygen. He squeezed his eyes closed, heightening every noise around him. At the first sign of trouble, Torch would yell the code word and they'd make a break for it.

One of the front wheels squeaked on Torch's old cleaning cart. There was a soft knock. Another. And another. The door to Chain Reaction's hospital room opened. "Who are you and what do you want?" growled a low voice.

"Need to clean," Torch said.

The crinkling of a piece of paper. "This room isn't supposed to be cleaned until tonight," another guard said.

"I was told that the person inside crapped in their bed. Gotta clean it up."

A pause. "Okay," another low voice said. "But be quick about it."

The cart's squeaky wheel started up, but the first guard spoke. "Hold on," he said.

"What are you doing?" Torch said, his voice cracking.

"What does it look like I'm doing, moron?" Something—probably a billy club—knocked against the cart with low thuds. "Open it up."

Strike squeezed his eyes even tighter, blood pounding in his head. He balled up his hands into fists, ready to squirt out of his hiding place and run like frakkin' hell.

"Open the door?" Torch asked. "Why?"

"Rules. Everything coming into this room gets inspected."

"But it's just cleaning supplies. I have to clean."

"Don't make me repeat myself. Open it, or I open your head."

"Sorry, sorry," Torch said. He fumbled with the door latch. He flipped it a few times, the latch snapping back into place each time. "Sweaty," he said. "I should get to work before—"

The billy club thwacked. Torch yelled out, then

groaned. The latch of the cart flipped and the door creaked open.

Strike cracked his eyes, squinting at the scene from his place inside a vent in the corner of the room. Torch was doubled over, holding his stomach, his face twisted in agony. The Blackguard had stuck his billy club inside the cart, clanging it around the vast array of buckets, brushes, and rags. He got to his knees, looking closely at the contents, going through every single item before grunting. "Stupid junker," he said. "Be quick about it. Clean up that crap before I rub your face in it." The guards left the room, slamming the door behind them.

Torch kept his eyes averted as he forced himself to straighten up. The hospital room was spotless, spacious by moon standards, with a curtain pulled back in one corner. Machines beeped, electronic equipment flashing all sorts of numbers. A security camera hung from the ceiling.

He whistled a nervous tune as he took out a rag and spray bottle. Washing down the surfaces of the walls, he glanced up toward the security camera and cocked his head. "Dusty," he said, seemingly to himself. Pulling over a chair, he got up onto it and wiped the walls around the camera, easing his way up toward it. He slowly dragged his rag over the camera's lens and held it there while knocking on the wall twice with his other hand. His eyes darted to the vent where Strike was hiding, the cover a meter above the floor.

Strike eased the metal vent cover out, centimeter by centimeter. And then it started to drop.

Torch squeezed his eyes closed tight, bracing himself for the disaster to come.

But all remained quiet. Strike had lunged forward into the room, catching the cover just before it clattered to the floor, which would have brought Blackguards running.

Strike popped his head out of the vent. After barely squeezing his way through the ductwork from a neighboring janitor's closet, he had come way too close to blowing the entire plan.

Torch motioned with his eyes toward the drawn curtain. He couldn't keep the rag in front of the camera for much longer without drawing suspicion.

Strike quickly wriggled out of the opening and jammed the vent cover back into place. He raced to the curtain, slipping behind it.

Torch started up a loud vacuum cleaner, creating a noisy background that would allow Strike to grill Chain Reaction unnoticed.

Strike's five minutes had begun.

His heart still racing from almost letting the vent cover clatter to the ground, Strike froze at the horrible sight in front of him. Chain Reaction was lying in a hospital bed, near death. Raw, oozing sores bloomed everywhere. Big swaths of his skin were peeling off. He reeked of decay, his flesh rotting. This couldn't be the brash Chain Reaction who had set so many Ultraball records. It couldn't be the same rocketback who could outleap anyone, outrun anyone.

This boy was a corpse.

Chain Reaction's eyelids fluttered at the sound of the vacuum cleaner humming in the background. He took a rattling breath that sounded like the Grim Reaper was giving him the kiss of death. Something caught in his lungs as he struggled to tilt his head up. Blinking himself into consciousness, he parted his cracked lips, a trail of blood crusted down his chin. "Strike?" he asked. "Is that really you?"

"What the frak happened to you?" Strike asked. "You look terrible."

"Yup, that's the Strike I know," Chain Reaction said in a bare whisper. "A total frakkin' idiot."

Strike winced at his stupidity. This was not the way to get someone to talk. "Sorry. I just meant . . . well . . ."

"I know," Chain Reaction said. "I don't look so hot, do I?" He managed a weak grin. The skin on his face was paper-thin, a patchwork of crackling scales.

"Is it true that Zuna can enlarge Ultrabot suits?" Strike blurted out. He knew he had to focus these precious minutes on Operation Deathstrike, but he couldn't stop himself. "He got you two extra seasons. How did he open up your suit?"

Chain Reaction pulled back another tired smile, showing off a mouthful of missing teeth. "Two extra seasons. I made myself a legend. The best rocketback of all time."

"Tell me how he enlarged your Ultrabot suit. Please. I have to know."

Chain Reaction let out a pathetic laugh that morphed into a fit of coughing. "As stupid as ever. Too bad your pal Rock isn't here. He'd have already figured it out."

"Figured what out?" Strike said. "Tell me. One Ultraball player to another. I'm begging you."

Chain Reaction rolled his eyes, wincing in pain with the effort. "Raiden Zuna isn't an engineer. He's a specialist in nuclear energy."

"What does that have to do with Ultrabot suits . . ." Strike trailed off, choking back his revulsion. "He nuked you?" Waves of horror crashed over him. "So you'd stop growing?"

"Took you long enough to figure it out, dummy," Chain Reaction said.

"But how did he force you to do it? Did he tie you down?"

"Man, you're the stupidest person on the moon." Chain Reaction slowly raised his arms, staring up at the ceiling. "I had no fear. I looked straight into the nuclear spear as it bathed me in its glory."

Recoiling, Strike took a step back. "You willingly did this? What were you thinking?"

"Isn't it obvious?"

Strike gaped in confusion.

"I did it for the glory," Chain Reaction said. "And that's what I got. I was the best rocketback the Underground Ultraball League will have ever seen. I will be remembered for all time. People will talk about me forever. I made myself immortal." He coughed, speckles of red spattering out.

Even five minutes ago, Strike would have said he'd do anything to get an extra year of Ultraball. But Strike hadn't understood what "anything" looked like.

Chain Reaction was in agonizing pain. His time would soon be up.

It dawned upon Strike how much he had outside of Ultraball. He loved hanging out with Rock. With Pickaxe and Nugget. And TNT. Strike stole a glance back at the curtain when it fluttered—Torch's secret signal that Strike's time was halfway up. Strike jerked back to his mission. "What's Operation Deathstrike?" he asked. "Is it Zuna's plan to kill me if I don't give him Boom?"

A horrible grin spread across Chain Reaction's face. He remained silent.

"Tell me!" Strike said, clawing his fingernails into the hospital bedding. "It's not just me, is it? Is Zuna going to murder others, too, if I don't give up Boom?"

Chain Reaction chuckled. "You think so small, you pea-brained imbecile. Once Zuna wins his huge bets on the Neutrons this year, he's going to make his grand plan a reality. White Lightning is helping him see to that." He paused. "I'll tell you one last thing. But only if you do something for me."

"What?"

Chain Reaction stretched out and grabbed Strike's hand, his grip weak. "Promise you won't tell anyone what you saw today. The moon has to remember me as a super-star. As the greatest Ultraball player in the history of the game. Agreed?"

That seemed so meaningless, considering what it had cost Chain Reaction. But Strike nodded.

Chain Reaction looked to the ceiling, holding his hands up even higher this time, stretching toward the heavens. "Think big." He turned toward Strike, his monstrous smile spreading from ear to ear, breaking into laughter of the devil himself. "Now you have everything you need to know."

"What?" Strike pounded a fist onto the bed. Chain Reaction had taunted him all his career, but this was a whole new level. The cryptic puzzle was one last slap in the face from Chain Reaction, his final demonstration of his superiority over Strike. "What's the one last thing you were going to tell me? What is the Deathstrike Device? Where is White Lightning building it?"

"You best go figure it out, dummy," Chain Reaction said. The gruesome smile faded, a profound sadness settling in. "What I wouldn't give to be inside my Ultra-bot suit one last time." With a rasping cough, he let his arms fall back down. "See you on the other side, Strike."

"Wait, you have to tell me—"

The curtain rustled again. Torch ducked his head in, fear in his eyes.

Although he knew he had to hurry, Strike couldn't help but stare at Chain Reaction, trying to sort through everything he had just heard. He took a last glimpse at the dying boy before nodding at Torch.

The two guards burst into the hospital room. "What are you doing?" one said, his billy club pointed at Torch.

Strike held his breath as he peered through the vent slits from inside his hiding place.

"Just cleaning! Don't hurt me!" Torch held his rag and spray bottle in front of his face. Averting his eyes, he dropped his gaze to the floor.

The two Blackguards scanned the room, one of them going straight to the camera. He got up on a chair and leaned in close, squinting. "Why were you wiping down this camera for so long?"

"Me?" Torch asked. He cocked his head, desperately trying to look brain-dead. "I'm supposed to clean the room."

"The security camera, too?" The Blackguard spent a few more seconds inspecting it. He adjusted it, tilting it back toward the center of the room, and then stepped off the chair. He got up into Torch's face. "I'll ask you one more time. What were you doing with that security camera?"

Torch let his mouth hang dumbly open. "I'm supposed to clean the room."

"Why do I even bother?" the Blackguard said. He joined his partner in scouring the rest of the room. One of the guards looked around the curtain, squinching up his face at the sight of Chain Reaction, as if he had just spotted a pile of dung. The other one slowly walked around the room, ending up at the vent near the floor. He bent down, peering through the metal slats.

Torch remained still, but tremors shook his hands. He shoved them into his pockets, balling them up into fists.

The Blackguard got to his knees, pulling at the vent cover. He banged it once with his billy club. "Loose," he said. Motioning to his partner, he waved him toward the door. "Snake it out, all the way to the other side of this vent path. Make sure the janitor's closet on the other side is clear."

Strike held his breath, trembling.

"What?" the other guard said. "Why?"

"Zuna's orders," the first guy said. "Secure all possible entrances and exits. Go."

On his way toward the door, the second guy shoved Torch. "What are you still doing here? Get out."

"I'm supposed to clean the room," Torch said. He pointed his rag at a dirty spot on the floor.

The Blackguard drew out his billy club and raised it. "You already said that, you dumb frakkin'—"

"Forget about it," the first Blackguard said. "The guy's a dimwit." He motioned toward the door with his club. "Get out before I crack open your frakkin' skull."

Torch nodded, shoving his cart hard, throwing all his weight behind it to get it into motion. The rickety wheel squeaked loudly as the cart slowly started to roll. He headed out the door and turned the corner into the hallway.

Inside the cramped cart, Strike's heart raced. With each step Torch took, he felt sure that the two Blackguards would come charging at them.

Torch took ten steps, his breathing strained and raggedy. Twenty steps. Thirty. Forty. He turned a corner and pushed the cart down a long hallway. After stealing a final glance over his shoulder, he pushed the squeaky cart toward the hospital's main door, and walked right by the guards at the exit.

14

ROCKETBACK 1

CHAIN REACTION'S CRYPTIC comments and gestures had haunted Strike for days. Not even Rock had been able to figure out what they meant. Whatever Chain Reaction was tormenting him with, it held the key to Operation Deathstrike. This was Chain Reaction's ultimate taunt, his crowning achievement in a lifetime of jeering and jabbing, asserting his dominance over Strike at every turn. Strike could still picture Chain Reaction, laughing maniacally at Strike's complete inability to decode the puzzle, even as the boy was slowly eroding into a corpse.

Rock had focused in on something Chain Reaction had said: *You think so small, you pea-brained imbecile. Think big.*

An inkling of what that could mean had begun to dawn on them, especially given what Zuna had said about wiping the moon of all its filth. But Strike couldn't bear to face the magnitude of that idea:

What if the Deathstrike Device is a weapon of mass murder, to be aimed at the Dark Siders?

And the definitive knowledge that there was no way to enlarge an Ultrabot suit hung heavy over Strike. He'd been so sure that he'd find an answer. Now, all he could do was bide his time until his number 8 suit would no longer close up around him, slamming the coffin door on his Ultraball career.

But as huge as those problems were, there was something even more pressing on Strike's mind. The Miners sat inside the locker room before their week-seven game against the Tranquility Beatdown. TNT was at the end of a bench, his arms folded across his chest as he scowled at Strike. The rest of the team was quiet, bystanders to the icy staring match.

Finally, Strike could take it no longer. "I know I owe you my life," he said. "I'll never forget that. But I can't put you back in yet. You're not fully healed."

"So what if I'm not?" TNT said. "Even if I was only at fifty percent—and I'm a lot higher than that—I'm still better than most of the rocketbacks out there." He kept his gaze trained on Strike, but he stole the slightest of glances at Nitro, who sat quietly on the other end of the bench. "Nothing personal against Nitro. But we have to do everything we can to win this game. I have to make things right with everyone in Taiko Colony. For what I did two years ago."

"I know how much that means to you," Strike said. "But you have to let it drop. Our fans have already forgiven you. Everyone knows that you took a knife for me. Now that's sacrifice." He looked to Nitro. "Speaking of forgiveness and sacrifice, Torch has more than made up for last year now. Both you and TNT have let go of the past. What's important is the future. Winning the Ultrabowl."

Nitro turned away. The way her face usually hardened upon hearing her brother's name was easing. After the great lengths Torch had taken to help out Strike, she had to forgive him. But it still tortured her.

"I have to do this," TNT said. "Please, Strike. I personally have to make things right."

"What do you want me to do?" Strike said. He got to his feet. "Look at how well Nitro has been playing."

"I should step aside," Nitro said. "It's the right thing to do."

"See, she doesn't even want to play," TNT said. "Back at Kamar station, you had to beg her to step in."

Strike studied Nitro. The idea that someone might not want to suit up was crazy, especially considering that he had no choice about his own Ultraball days being numbered. But as recently as three weeks ago, Nitro had told TNT that she couldn't wait until he was ready to take back his roster spot. "Do you actually want to play?"

She looked nervously at TNT, then nodded. "More than anything," she said. "I admit, I hated the idea at first. And when I had all those fumbles, I've never felt worse in my entire life. Not even when Torch told me what he did last year." She stood up a little straighter. "But things are different now. I've worked so hard on my game. I love that feeling of my suit closing up around me, transforming me into a mech weapon. I love Ultraball. I've never loved anything more."

"Berzerkatron says she's in the running for MVP," Strike said. "I can't take her out. As the coach of the Miners, I have to field the team that I think has the best shot at winning."

"The best shot at winning the Ultrabowl," TNT said. "That means me. I may not be fully healed up yet, but I will be by the time the Ultrabowl rolls around. The team needs time to get used to the old lineup again."

"We have to make it to the Ultrabowl first," Strike countered. He took a deep breath, trying to tamp down the rage that was rising inside him. "Look. I'll get you worked back onto the roster next week for the semis. But today, we have to focus on taking down the Beatdown. They're going to be fierce. We have to win, and win big.

We cannot fall into the fourth seed."

"All the more reason to put me in," TNT said. "I've played the Beatdown. I know how to use the giant boulders on the field. I have experience. That counts for a lot."

Everyone looked up at the speaker mounted overhead as the announcers started their pregame chatter.

"Just a couple of minutes left to turn in a roster change," TNT said. "What's it going to be?"

"Don't pressure me," Strike said. "I—"

"Take me out," Rock said.

Everyone turned toward him, the room falling silent except for the banter of Berzerkatron and the Mad Mongol on the overhead speakers.

"It's the only move that makes sense," Rock continued. "I've always been the weakest rocketback on the team. In the league. We'd have a much better shot at the title with TNT and Nitro as our rocketbacks." He got to his feet and went over to his number 5 Ultrabot suit. "We've had quite a run together. But she's yours now, TNT."

"Whoa, whoa," TNT said. "I appreciate the offer, but I can't take your spot."

"You have to," Rock said.

TNT shook his head, crossing his arms tight. "I won't do it."

"Then I quit," Rock said. He turned to Strike. "Now you have no choice but to put TNT in."

"Everybody just hang on a minute," Strike said. "Let me think."

"There's nothing to think about," Rock said. "The logical decision is to insert TNT into the roster alongside Nitro. They're both better rocketbacks than I am."

"What about team chemistry?" Nugget said. "It takes a while for a new roster to gel."

"Yeah," Pickaxe added. "Look what happened in Nitro's first two games."

"It took me three games, plus the constant fumble drills, to get into the swing of things," Nitro said. She interlaced her fingers, squeezing them together, her knuckles white with the strain. "I think you guys ought to go back to the Fireball Five lineup. That's a known quantity."

Strike held up his hands, trying to keep the pressure at bay. "Can everyone just be quiet for a second?" he said.

Rock looked up at the clock mounted high on the wall. "I don't mean to rush you, but any final roster changes have to be submitted in the next five minutes. That's barely enough time to get to the announcers' booth."

Strike took a deep breath. He gave TNT the stink-eye before taking out the team's roster form and slowly filling it out. He folded it in half and then handed it to Rock.

The Miners lined up just inside the tunnel as the announcers prepared to introduce the visiting team into

Beatdown Arena. At the front of the line, Strike turned to give everyone a final nod.

Nitro and TNT stood at the back of the line, both of them restless, on edge. TNT raised a thumbs-up sign and forced out a smile.

The announcer called out Strike's name, and he raced forward. An immediate chorus of boos came raining down on him like an avalanche of rocks. Pickaxe came out next, followed by Nugget, and then Nitro, each one greeted by a similar round of jeers from the crowd filled mostly with fans wearing the purple jumpsuits of Tranquility Colony.

The world seemed to stop when TNT's name was announced. The stadium quickly filled with a low buzz of confusion. Then the boos rained down once again. TNT raised his arms, goading on the crowd. "It's great to be back," he yelled into the Miners' helmet comm. "I've even missed the booing."

The Miners huddled up as the announcers shifted to the home team, everyone in the arena jumping to their feet as the Beatdown raced in through their tunnel. Takedown. Chokehold. Hammer Fist, who seemed to be limping. Uppercut. And their quarterback, Destroyer. The five members of the Tranquility Beatdown had played together for years now, and their chemistry burned bright as the five purple-suited players chest-bumped and whooped it up in perfect coordination.

Chemistry isn't all that important, Strike willed himself to believe.

"Set up for the kickoff return," he said into the Miners' helmet comm. "Black hole fifty-four."

The Miners strode to their end zone with Strike in the left side of the field. TNT and Nitro bumped into each other as they both headed to the rocketback 1 position on the right side of the field. "Oops," Nitro said. "Sorry."

"It's okay," TNT said. He pointed over to the rocketback 2 spot behind him. "Maybe you'll earn the 1 spot one day." He threw her a grin, but she didn't smile back.

"Cut her some slack, big shot," Pickaxe said. "She's been our go-to player for the past two games. You can't just waltz in and take your spot back."

"Whoa," TNT said. "I was just kidding around. Trying to lighten things up. Nitro's done a great job at rocketback 1. She and I are going to blow up the Beatdown. Together."

Strike furrowed his forehead, keeping his eyes trained on the Beatdown, five players in gleaming purple looking to put the hurt on the Miners. On paper, this lineup gave the Miners their best chance of winning. Rock might actually be more valuable as a coach than a player, too, able to analyze every little detail as the game unfolded, helping them make critical corrections. But it felt so wrong that their steadiest and most consistent player—part of the Miners' very foundation—wasn't suited up. Strike glanced to the stands at their coach's box, where Rock was huddled over his notebook, scribbling madly into it.

A ref in black plate armor blew a whistle, and the Beatdown sprinted forward, the kickoff man slamming his boot into the Ultraball. But instead of kicking it high into the air, it came shooting like a missile down the field, just a meter above the turf.

"Incoming," Strike yelled. "Charge." He raced forward, accelerating to full speed in a few steps, his boots clomping into blurs of motion. The other Miners flanked him, and they sped along in a tight wedge formation.

"Wait," Rock's voice chimed in, loud over helmet comm. "Spread out. It's headed toward boulder four."

Strike turned briefly to catch sight of Rock in the stands, jumping up and down in the Miners' coach's box. "Spread delta blue," he yelled to the others. The other Miners broke off at different angles to fan out.

A second later, the Ultraball blasted into a giant boulder on the thirty-meter line, cracking it apart with a thunderous boom. Pieces of rock went flying in all directions. A cloud of gray dust burst out, and Strike lost the Ultraball in the confusion. Scanning his heads-up display, he picked up the blinking red dot. "TNT, your side!"

TNT was already on an intercept course. He threw himself at the bouncing Ultraball, snatching it off the turf. The ball locked into his magnetic glove, but as he tried to switch it from his left to right hand, he bobbled it. A Beatdown defender smashed into TNT. The ball popped straight up into the air.

The defender leapt for the Ultraball, stretching to full extension. He locked the ball into one of his gloves, but TNT came in swinging wildly, one of his punches knocking it out. The ball took an awkward bounce, and TNT leapt on it.

"Lateral!" Nitro yelled. She was toward the other side of the field, holding her hands up, ready to catch a pass and take off.

TNT popped to his feet, ducking just in time to avoid a Beatdown defender flying at his head. As another defender charged at him, TNT whirled and heaved the ball across the field to Nitro. But the lateral was low and behind her. She slid to a halt and doubled back to get to it, barely snagging it near the tips of her boots. That was all it took to enable a Beatdown defender to catch up to her, locking a glove onto her Ultrabot suit. He dragged her to the turf, trying to slam the ball out of her grasp, but Nitro held on tight. The rest of the Beatdown came in to smother her at the forty-meter line.

"Tough throw," Strike said as he held out a hand to pull TNT up.

TNT's helmet visor was on reflective mode, but Strike could almost see the wince of pain as he got to his feet. "Just a little rusty, that's all. I'll be fine."

"Okay," Strike said. "Huddle it up." He tried to listen over the helmet comm as Rock relayed in a play from the sidelines, but it was hard to concentrate. At his best, TNT was a one-man wrecking crew, a weapon who could tear up the league. How long was it going to take him to get back there?

"Did you hear me?" Rock said over helmet comm.

"What?" Strike asked. "Yes. What did you say?"

"Avalanche two, fly intercept," Rock repeated.

Strike thought about Rock's call: a long bomb to a streaking TNT. Nitro would be in the middle of the field, waiting to heave a giant boulder at TNT's defender as he passed. It might be brilliant, but it could be a disaster. "No," he said. "Sharpshooter shield to TNT. Let's work him in a little easier."

"I'm okay," TNT said. "Turn me loose. Avalanche two, fly. It'll be an easy catch when my man gets blasted by Nitro. Right?" He flipped his visor to clear, nodding at Nitro.

"I'll do whatever I'm asked, for the good of the team," Nitro said, her visor still set to reflective.

"Run avalanche two, fly intercept," Rock said over helmet comm. "It's the best percentage play."

For years, Strike had called every single play for the Miners. It was weird having someone chirp play calls into his ear, even if that person was his best friend and one of the smartest people on the moon. "Time's running down," he said. "Sharpshooter shield, on two. Set it up."

Nugget dutifully got into position over the Ultraball, Strike setting up right behind him. Pickaxe lined up wide, right next to a giant boulder numbered with a huge five. TNT and Nitro both retreated into the deep backfield, hiding behind boulder number eight.

Strike eyed the Beatdown defenders, two of them stacked right at the line, twitching, ready to take off at Strike and spear him with everything they had. "Make it happen, TNT," he said. "Nitro, give him protection. Hut hut!"

Nugget hiked the ball to Strike, who scrambled backward, ducking as one of the defenders hurdled over Nugget to launch himself at Strike. With a quick spin, Strike evaded the defender and scrambled right.

At the same time, TNT came flying over the boulder he had been hiding behind, charging upfield. He slammed a defender off his feet and crossed the line of scrimmage. Strike zipped him a hard pass, the ball clanging against TNT's chest plate as he snagged it at full speed. With Pickaxe as his lead blocker, TNT took off.

A Beatdown defender smashed into Pickaxe, knocking both of them into a heap. Another defender shot in and latched a magnetic glove onto TNT's boot, tripping him up. The Beatdown man almost reeled in TNT, but Nitro heaved a giant boulder into both of them, smashing them to the side. The defender slammed to the ground, and his grip on TNT popped loose. TNT stumbled as he got up, looking around in a state of disorientation. He ran toward the corner of the end zone, more in a zigzag than a straight line.

"Look out!" Strike yelled over helmet comm.

TNT was at the fifteen-meter line when a shadow grew around him. He looked up and cried out, just before an enormous boulder plummeted onto him, smashing him to the ground.

Whistles blew as refs came in to untangle the pileup. One of them carried a maglev lift that he used to roll the boulder off TNT.

As soon as he was free, TNT popped to his feet, yelling at Nitro. "Why the frak did you throw that boulder at me so hard?"

Nitro took a step back at first, but stopped, holding her ground. "I got you free of your guy," she said. "That was my job, and I did it." She kept her visor at reflective, letting her implication about TNT's failure hang heavy in the air.

"Quit it, both of you," Strike said. "Set up for the next play or we'll have to take our time-out." He looked over to Nitro, who walked away from TNT, her body language showing her frustration with the Miners' rocketback 1. Then he trained his gaze on TNT, not sure which of the two he should be yelling at.

Strike knew TNT all too well. TNT's eruption of

anger at Nitro was just a front. The person he was really mad at was himself.

The old TNT would have scored that touchdown ten out of ten times, Strike thought.

RESULTS, WEEK 7

Miners	**91**
Beatdown	84
Molemen	**70**
Venom	0
Neutrons	**140**
Shock	21
Flamethrowers	**91**
Explorers	84

STANDINGS, WEEK 7

	Wins	Losses	Total Points
1-Neutrons	6	1	749
2-Miners	5	2	595
3*-Beatdown	5	2	546
4*-Molemen	5	2	546
Flamethrowers	4	3	518
Explorers	2	5	469
Shock	1	6	350
Venom	0	7	203

Tiebreaker based on head-to-head record

PLAYOFF SEEDINGS

1	Neutrons (at Neutron Stadium)
4	Molemen
2	Miners (at Taiko Arena)
3	Beatdown

WRAITHS AND GHOSTS

It had been months since Strike had been to the junk pile outside of Taiko Colony. It had once been his and TNT's secret place, their private clubhouse. Open to anyone who wanted to go there, it wasn't secure at all. But no one else was crazy enough to go to the most foul-smelling place on the moon. He sat on the edge of the enormous sloping hole, staring into the depths of the ooze, hoping that Wraith would show up. He'd been over Chain Reaction's cryptic comments hundreds of times, and the solution to the puzzle had finally come together. Strike had to find a way to warn Boom about what was coming: a full-scale attack on the Dark Side of the moon.

He jerked his head to his right when a piece of trash

moved. His breathing ragged and shallow, he forced himself to chuckle. *Nothing's down there*, he thought. *Just my stupid imagination.*

"What are you laughing at?" came a whisper from the spot where the trash had moved.

Strike jumped back in terror, scrabbling at the ground in a frantic attempt to run away. He nearly screamed when the voice hissed out, "Stop. It's me."

Strike forced himself to halt and look back. Even squinting, he didn't believe his eyes. "Wraith?"

A figure emerged from the hole, covered with garbage, smeared with putrid goo. "Did anyone follow you?" Wraith asked. She wiped her eyes with the back of her hand, but it hardly did anything to remove the sludge coating her face.

"Why are you down in there?" Strike asked.

"A better question: Why aren't you down here?" she asked.

"Because it's disgusting?"

"Better than being caught." She attempted to shake something brown off her shoulder. "It sure is nasty, though."

"Don't worry, no one but you and me are stupid enough to come here," Strike said. "Thanks for showing up."

"This better be worth the tremendous risk we're taking. I barely shook Zuna's flunkies in order to get here. You have something important I need to know about?"

Strike told her everything that had happened when he had snuck into Salaam Hospital. His memory usually wasn't that reliable, but every detail of those five minutes had been burned into his brain. There was no way he could ever forget the horrible, sickly grin on Chain Reaction's face as he raised his arms to the ceiling.

Wraith took it all in, listening carefully. "Are you sure you're not missing something he said about this Death-strike Device?" she asked. "All he did was raise his arms and look up high?"

"Trust me, I've been over it a hundred times," Strike said. "He's always loved to taunt me."

"What could he have meant about Zuna's grand plan?" Wraith asked.

Chain Reaction's words flashed into Strike's head. *Once Zuna wins his huge bets on the Neutrons this year, he's going to make his grand plan a reality.* That could only mean one thing. "He's going to kill everyone on the Dark Side," Strike said. "Maybe he's going to secretly mount nukes to the ceilings of your caverns."

"He can't even get to the Dark Side, at least without us knowing about it immediately."

"What else would he be talking about when he said he was going to wipe the moon of all its filth? You have to warn Boom and everyone else."

Wraith didn't argue with him. Instead, a fierce determination burned in her eyes. "One of us must stop the

Neutrons from winning the Ultrabowl. It has to be my Molemen or your Miners." She gave him a crooked grin. "Good thing my team fell into the fourth seed, huh?"

"So it's true?" Strike asked. *LunarSports Reports* had jumped all over the Molemen for supposedly halting their scoring on purpose in a crooked scheme to drop into the fourth seed. Wraith had denied it all, but now Strike saw her genius at work.

"This way, I have the first shot at stopping Zuna," Wraith said. "And if he pulls more of his underhanded tricks to somehow beat us, you'll still be able to take down the Neutrons in the Ultrabowl."

"Tricks? What tricks?"

"You think the Beatdown's roster issue is accidental? Hammer Fist having stomach trouble, two games in a row? Can't be a coincidence."

Strike's eyes widened. "Hammer Fist is taking a payoff from Zuna?"

"No. I think he's being poisoned. I'd bet a thousand U-bucks that it'll happen again."

The horror of it all trickled through Strike like a deadly virus. *LunarSports Reports* had reported that Hammer Fist's stomach problems were due to the intense pressure getting to him. But Wraith's explanation made way more sense.

"Even if Hammer Fist gets mysteriously sick again, the Beatdown are going to be tough to get past," Wraith said.

She raised her eyebrows at Strike. "You have to do something about your roster."

Strike picked up a pebble and tossed it up a few times before chucking it into the giant junk hole. It sailed down, landing with a plop into something goopy.

"Are you listening to me?" Wraith said.

"The roster is fine. It was rough at first, but TNT and Nitro gelled in the second half."

"You're deluding yourself. If you guys play like you did in your last game, there's no way you're going to win. The Beatdown are going to destroy you."

Strike spat out his words. "What the frak am I supposed to do? On paper, TNT and Nitro should be the best rocketback 1 and 2 combo out there."

"The game isn't played on paper."

"Okay, fine," Strike yelled. "We have a problem. And I have no idea how to fix it." He squeezed his eyes tight in frustration. "What would you do?"

"I don't know all your team dynamics," Wraith said. She paused, considering her words. "But I think you gotta get Rock back in your lineup."

Strike took a deep breath, chewing at the inside of his mouth. That thought had bounced in and out of his head for days now. If there was one thing the Miners needed, it was stability.

"Rock definitely isn't one of the best rocketbacks in

the game," Wraith continued, "but he does the things a team needs. All the stuff that goes unnoticed. Blocks and pressured throws that don't get counted in the stats. I think you've underestimated how important he is to—" She stopped abruptly and yanked Strike forward, throwing him into the junk pile.

Strike landed with a splat in a puddle of goo. "What the frak are you doing?" he said. His entire right side was covered in glop. Disgusted, he tried to shake some of it off, but there was nastiness smeared all over him. "Are you crazy?"

"Shh," Wraith hissed. She poked her head over the rim of the deep pit and pointed toward the main entrance.

The airlock door started to slide back. Strike's eyes widened as four Blackguards crept in, all with their billy clubs out, held at the ready.

"We know you're in there," one of the Blackguards called out. "Come out peacefully and there will be no trouble. But we will use force if necessary."

Strike watched as the Blackguards edged closer. "We should do what they say," he whispered. "We haven't done anything wrong."

"You think they'll just question us a little and let us go?" Wraith said. "Think about what they did to Fusion. To Hammer Fist. They might even be the ones who attacked you at Kamar Colony." Wraith shook her head.

"I should never have come. We're trapped."

Strike wanted to smash himself in the head. "I'm such a moron," he whispered. His mind raced as he spotted two more Blackguards emerging through the airlock door. "I'm going to turn myself in. I can't be responsible for you getting captured. You run."

"Don't be a fool," Wraith said. "I have to protect you. You're too important to the rebellion."

"I'm not that important. The rebellion—"

"You *are* the rebellion," Wraith said. "It fails without you." She pointed to the airlock door, the lone entrance and exit. "Where do you think I would run, anyway? Just waltz right by the Blackguards?"

There was no other exit. The Blackguards silently closed in on them. Maybe they'd just be taken in for questioning. But deep down, Strike knew that Wraith was right. The junk pile had no cameras, no recorders, no witnesses. Strike tensed his legs. If there was nothing he could do, he'd do something crazy. Maybe racing at the Blackguards would give Wraith enough of a distraction to somehow slip out the airlock door.

"Stop that," Wraith said, putting a hand on his shoulder and shoving him down. "Hold still. We have a plan." She shot a glance over her left shoulder, holding a hand up with all five fingers outstretched.

"Who's back there?" Strike asked.

"Quiet," Wraith said. Her gaze was fixed upon the Blackguards, who were edging closer and closer. When they were just ten meters away, she silently counted down by curling down one finger at a time. When she reached a closed fist, she yelled, "Now!"

Strike instinctively ducked as trash went flying all around him. Dark Siders in dirty white jumpsuits exploded out of their hiding places, buried under the surface of the junk pile, heaving sticky clods of garbage at the Blackguards as they charged. The cavern erupted in chaos, Blackguards storming toward the junk hole, billy clubs swinging away. One smashed into a Dark Sider's head with a horrible *thunk*, and the man reeled. His knees buckled, the lifeless mass crumpling to the ground.

"Go!" Wraith yelled. She grabbed the back of Strike's jumpsuit, yanking him to his feet. "Get him out of here!" Two big Dark Siders ran up behind Strike, grabbing his arms.

Strike tried to stop himself, to stay and fight alongside Wraith. But the Dark Siders were too strong, lifting him clear off the ground, his feet tripping along as they hauled him toward the airlock door. "Let me go," he screamed, struggling in vain to break free.

A Blackguard raced to intercept, but one of the Dark Siders jerked low to duck the billy club swing aimed at his head. He let go of Strike and threw a rabbit punch into the Blackguard's stomach. The Blackguard fell backward, holding his gut, moaning. The Dark Siders picked Strike back up and sprinted toward the exit.

Two more Blackguards followed in hot pursuit, closing the distance quickly. One of the Dark Siders dropped Strike's arm, staying back to intercept the attackers while the other one carried Strike toward the airlock door, ignoring his protests that he needed to stay and fight.

The first Dark Sider dropped down and swept his leg low as a Blackguard came at him, tripping him. But the other Blackguard kicked out, cracking his boot into the Dark Sider's shoulder, knocking him backward to the ground. He raised his billy club and thwacked it into the Dark Sider's legs and torso, the Dark Sider screaming with each blow.

Strike and his Dark Sider escort were nearly at the airlock door when the nearest Blackguard threw his billy club at them. It cracked into the Dark Sider's back, making him lurch forward. He slammed to the ground, right on top of Strike.

All the air exploded out of Strike's lungs as the Dark Sider landed on him. He sucked desperately for air, but nothing came. Red stars exploded around the periphery of his vision. He tried to curl up into a ball until his lungs started working again. But the Dark Sider had already slung him over his shoulder and sprinted the last steps to the exit. He kicked the button to open the door. As soon as it slid wide open enough, he tossed Strike through it, sending him sliding to the ground on the other side. "Run!" he yelled.

"I can't abandon Wraith," Strike said.

"We'll take care of her. You have to get to safety, or all of this will be for nothing." Slapping the button on the control panel, he raced back into the fight.

The door reversed, slowly inching its way closed. Torn, Strike watched the battle happening by the edge of the pit. The Dark Siders were overpowering the Blackguards, the element of surprise heavily on their side. But two Blackguards were still swinging away, each crazed blow backed by the frenzy and raw power that came from desperation. One of them suddenly turned and charged at Wraith, who was helping subdue another Blackguard on the ground.

"Wraith, look out!" Strike yelled, jabbing a finger through the still closing doors.

She jerked around, ducking the Blackguard's wild attack just in time, the billy club whistling over her head. But the next blow came too fast, cracking into her shoulder with a horrible thud. Screaming, she collapsed, clawing at her shoulder in agony.

Two Dark Siders came in and tackled the Blackguard, stripping his billy club away and wrenching his arm behind his back. One of them turned toward the airlock door, spotting Strike peering dumbly through the doors that were nearly closed now. "Run, you fool! More will be coming!"

The doors slid shut.

Strike ran.

The Lunar World News *Postgame Report*

"This is Aziz Chang, here with Lunar World News's newest member, Beastfire, formerly of the Touchdown Zone. It is such an honor having one of the most famous people on the moon by my side, the MVP of Ultrabowls IV and V, the spitfire, live wire, highflier, Beastfire. How you doin', Beast?"

"I'm awesome, now that I'm working for LWN, the newest and already most watched source of news across the moon. I ain't gonna hold no punches as I light up the straight dope on Ultraball. Beastfire goin' haywire!"

"Excellent. Let's get right down to the semifinals action. The North Pole Neutrons have advanced to their fifth straight Ultrabowl, after pounding the Cryptomare Molemen, 77–56. In a bizarre move, the Molemen made a surprise roster change just before the start of the game. Taking Wraith out of the lineup, they shifted Smuggler to quarterback, Cutter to rocketback 1, and inserted a rookie named Burial at rocketback 2. The moves drew huge skepticism from color commentators around the moon, speculating on the Molemen's motives. The Underground Ultraball League has initiated a full investigation. Your thoughts, Beast?"

"That's some screwy stuff, all right. Wraith sittin'

up in the Molemen's coach's box during the game, not speaking to anyone around her? She didn't even make herself available for the mandatory postgame press conference. Even this dummy knows that 'mandatory' means you gotta do it. The question on everyone's mind: What is she hidin'? She part of some crooked scheme, placing bets against her own team? Probbly. Don't forget that she purposefully dropped her team from the third to the fourth seed, most likely because she had money ridin' on it. She could be up to something even more illegaler than that."

"She appeared to be limping, favoring her right arm as she left the stands after the game. Do you believe the rumors that she was injured and couldn't play?"

"No frakkin' way. Ultraball is war. Ain't no thing as injured. Until that suit don't close up around you no more, you play, no matter what. You're in an indestructible suit, for frak's sake! You go out and you frakkin' play."

"Excellent points, B-Fire. Meanwhile, in the other semifinal game, the Miners squeaked by the Beatdown, barely surviving a last-second scare to secure a 63–56 victory. Was it just me, or did the Miners look like a minor-league team?"

"They's an embarrassment to Ultraball itself. It's disgusting. TNT and Nitro are an explosive pair—not in a good way. What a frakkin' mess. It ain't even worth playin' the Ultrabowl. It's just gonna be sad to watch the Neutrons whoop the Miners' bare butts."

"The oddsmakers heavily favor the Neutrons in the Ultrabowl, assigning them a seventy-eight percent chance of taking home their fifth straight title. What do you think about that number—too high, too low?"

"Lower than a Dark Sider's shadow. Don't forget, Nitro ain't got no playoff experience. Under the intense pressure of the moon's biggest stage, I bet her fumbleitis comes right back."

"Playoff experience. It's that important?"

"Course it is! Any frakhead knows that. The jump from regular season to the playoffs is massive. Just look at Torch. That dude had been playin' as incredulous as Nitro, back when he took his Flamethrowers all the way to Ultrabowl VI. But by throwing a fatal interception on the last play of the game, he demonstrated that rookies don't belong in no Ultrabowl. He's long been forgotten. Who knows where that sorry loser is now."

"Some say that Nitro is destined to follow in her brother's footsteps, the Torch's Curse now hexing the Miners. Would you say there's any truth to the Curse, Part II?"

"Frak yeah. The over/under for how many times she fumbles is set at 2.5. I say that's way, way, waaaay too low. I'm so sure of that, I bet ten thousand U-bucks on it."

"Ten thousand? Now, that's putting your money

where your mouth is. Speaking of betting, the total amount already wagered on the Ultrabowl is estimated to be seven hundred million U-dollars. The stakes have never been higher. Anything to add before we move to player interviews, B-Fire?"

"Gonna be a frakkin' crap Ultrabowl. Miners gonna get theyselves pounded. May as well not even suit up."

"There you have it, folks, you've heard it from the foremost Ultraball authority on the moon, the man blazing like a superstar supernova, the legendary two-time Ultrabowl MVP, Beastfire. The smart money— including B-Fire's—is on the Neutrons to take home their fifth straight Ultrabowl title, and for their dynasty to continue indefinitely."

ALL EYES ON STRIKE

IT HAD BEEN a hard-fought semifinals victory, the Miners barely edging out the Tranquility Beatdown in the last seconds of the punishing playoff game. Right afterward, the Miners entered their locker room, everyone clicking out of their Ultrabot suits and collapsing to benches in dead exhaustion. A win was a win, the Miners now advancing to their fifth Ultrabowl in a row. But this one had been a heart-stopping squeaker.

Strike slumped forward, wiping sweat off his brow. The Miners had caught a lucky break, the Beatdown forced to insert a rookie at rocketback 2 after Hammer Fist had become too sick to suit up. Even with that big advantage, though, there had been so many problems with the Miners' lineup.

There's no way we're going to win the Ultrabowl like this, he thought.

"Look," Rock said. He pointed to a screen mounted to the wall, the loudmouthed commentators chattering away, Beastfire holding court, the former Ultrabowl MVP mesmerizing everyone with his folksy banter.

Lunar World News was only weeks old, formed when Raiden Zuna bought the *Lunar Times* and combined it with *LunarSports Reports*, but it had already become the most-watched program on TV. The word "Exclusive" was now flashing in big red letters on the screen, *LWN* cutting to footage of reporters chasing Wraith as she limped away after the game. They kept lobbing questions at her with no response, until one asked, "Who's your pick in the Ultrabowl?"

Wraith turned, looking right into the camera. "The Miners will win. They have to." Dark Siders swarmed in to escort Wraith away. A contingent of Blackguards kept close to them.

"Someone turn off that frakkin' crap," Pickaxe said, lying down on a bench. "It's giving me a headache." He poked his brother, who was sprawled out next to him.

"You do it," Nugget said. "I'm so tired, not even your stench can budge me."

"Fine," Pickaxe said. He reached toward the screen and

grimaced, letting his arm fall to his side. "Frak. Beastfire is a big-mouthed goon, but maybe he's right."

Strike's stomach threatened to toss up the bitter hardtack bar he had choked down at halftime. His struggling Miners badly needed a pep talk to help build some confidence for the coming Ultrabowl. He got to his feet and turned off the TV. "Today was close," he said. "But we got through. The Neutrons next week . . . well, don't think about the past four years. All those losses don't mean a thing now."

TNT cleared his throat, a weak grin coming to his face. "I wasn't thinking about that until you reminded us," he said.

Everyone broke into nervous laughter, the tension cracking ever so slightly. Rock took out his notebook. "That goes under 'Jokes That Aren't Really Funny but Serve a Useful Purpose,'" he muttered to himself. The laughter increased, and Rock looked up in surprise. "What happened? What did I miss?"

"Nothing, buddy," TNT said. "You just did something great. We're going to go out and roll the Neutrons." His face fell. "I mean, you guys are. I quit."

Everyone went silent.

"Shut the frak up," Pickaxe said. "You can't quit."

"You're still an awesome rocketback," Nugget said.

"Fireball Five forever," Pickaxe said. He hesitated, then gave Nitro a friendly poke in the shoulder. "I gotta admit, Nitro is better than you right now, especially because of your injury. She is awesome. Carried us right into the playoffs. But you deserve the rocketback 1 spot. If you hadn't taken a knife for Strike back in Kamar Colony, you'd be a sure thing for MVP."

TNT took a deep breath, staring down. "About that." He ground his feet into the floor, chewing on his lip. "I wasn't trying to jump in. I just got caught in the mix." He peered up at Strike. "I wanted to tell you the truth. It just got out of hand before I could. Not that I wouldn't trade my life for yours. But Wraith was the one who saved you. Not me."

TNT let the admission sink in amid the stunned silence, and then smacked a locker door. "Even if I had been some kind of a hero, this is the only choice. Nitro and I, we don't mesh as rocketbacks. I should be the one to step down."

Nitro shook her head. "You have way more playoff experience. It should be you out there at rocketback 1." She thunked a fingertip into her chest. "Torch and me, maybe we are cursed. I dropped that pass at the start of the second half. Would have been a sure touchdown. It's only going to get worse next week, when the pressure's way higher."

"There is no such thing as a curse," Rock said.

"Enough," TNT said. He stood up and offered a handshake to Nitro. "You earned your spot, fair and square.

Frak, you can even throw better than me out of the rocket booster option. Better than Strike, even. Your arm is a cannon."

"There is an easy and logical solution to this dilemma," Rock said. "I'm not nearly as good a rocketback as either of you. I will continue to sit on the sideline so that both of you can play."

"No," TNT said. "We need your stabilizing influence on the field. You anchor everything. Without you, things are gonna continue to spiral out of control. Right, Coach?"

All faces turned to Strike, the room going quiet again. He froze at the sudden attention, realizing that he had been sitting back, hoping someone would make the decision for him. It felt like it wasn't just the eyes of his teammates locked onto him—it was the eyes of the moon.

TNT had worked so hard for redemption. At 100 percent, he was the best rocketback in the league, bar none. But there was no doubt that he was still suffering from his injury.

Then there was Nitro, who had exploded as a potential MVP candidate, spending so many hours practicing her fumble drills, carrying an Ultraball whenever she was suited up in order to cure her of her one glaring flaw. Was all the talk of the Curse, Part II, still haunting her, though?

And then Strike knew what he had to do. It was going to be the toughest week of his life. He took a deep breath, anticipating the pain and exhaustion that the coming days would bring for every single Miner. "Let's head back to Taiko Arena," he said. "We have a ton of work to do."

"Who's it going to be?" TNT asked.

Focusing on the door, Strike motioned everyone ahead. He bit his lip at the thought of what he was going to have to say to his teammates, struggling to figure out some way to break the news to everyone as gently as possible.

The Fireball Five had played their last Ultrabowl together.

STARTING LINEUP

BERZERKATRON'S AMPLIFIED VOICE filled Saladin Stadium. "Welcome, all, to the eleventh annual Ultrabowl, the biggest game of the year. Ultrabowl XI features yet another rematch of the perennial top dogs of the Underground Ultraball League. It is only fitting that they finished at the number one and two seeds at the end of the regular season. I hope you're ready for some lights-out Ultraball!

"Now, introducing this year's second seed. The team that has appeared in the past four Ultrabowls, but has lost each one in heartbreaking fashion. In the bright blue of Taiko Colony, with a regular season record of five wins and two losses, five hundred ninety-five total points scored over those games, I give you . . . the Taiko Miners!"

The crowd was mostly dressed in the red jumpsuits of North Pole Colony, but the few pockets of blue went berserk, jumping up and down, sending a wave of vibrations through the stands. Governor Katana was front and center at the fifty-meter line, surrounded by a pack of bodyguards. He forced out a smile when a camera trained on him, but the corners of his eyes were creased with lines of worry.

"Introducing the Miners' starting lineup. At crackback 2, in the Miners' number 9 Ultrabot suit, it's Nugget!"

A round of cheers went up as Nugget ran onto the turf and did a double backflip. He landed and immediately rebounded, jumping high into the sky and punching up a victorious fist.

"Joining his brother at crackback 1, locked into the blue number 7 Ultrabot suit, it's . . . Pickaxe!"

Another roar surged, Pickaxe eating it up as he raced toward his brother. Nugget charged back at him, and they both leapt into the air at the same time. They collided with a thunderous boom, locking arms together as they spun into a dizzying blur. They thudded back to the turf and both slammed punches into the ground.

"Next up, the Miners' rocketback 2. They call him their foundation, their steadiest player. Introducing Rock, in the number 5 Ultrabot suit!"

The crowd briefly went silent. Rock jogged out with

no swagger, no display of bravado, no nothing. Then a couple of polite cheers went up through the Miners' diehard fans, but it was far from wild. Some even booed.

Strike gritted his teeth. That was fine. The fans didn't have to like his decision right now, but they'd call him a genius when the Miners lifted the Ultrabowl trophy into the air.

"And at rocketback 1, holding some of the Underground Ultraball League records, including an incredible twelve touchdowns scored in a single game, in the number 3 Ultrabot suit . . . it's TNT!"

The pockets of Miners fans whipped into a frenzy once again, as TNT blasted out of the tunnel like a missile, just a blue blur shooting toward the other Miners. Pickaxe and Nugget stood a meter apart, each crackback catching one of TNT's arms as he raced in, and together, they slung him skyward. His momentum redirected, TNT flew all the way to the ceiling, cracking into it. He kicked off into a wild horizontal spin, his limbs sticking straight out as he whirled back to the turf like a helicopter blade. Rock caught him, and all four Miners punched their fists into the air at the same time.

The sins of TNT's past had been forgiven. If the Miners won, TNT's slate would not only be wiped clean: he'd be lionized for all time as one of the most famous people in the history of the moon.

"Finally, quarterbacking the Miners, in the number 8 Ultrabot suit, it's . . ."

The Miners on the field turned to look at the tunnel. Everyone in the stands focused in, too.

The announcer cleared his throat. "It's Nitro!"

The entire arena erupted in chaos. Nitro jogged out under the spotlights, her visor set to reflective. Like always, she carried her Ultraball tucked safely away, cradled into her left arm. She joined her teammates at the center of the field, high-fiving and butt-slapping, trying to ignore the roars of confusion and disbelief echoing through the stands. The Miners set up in a slingshot V. TNT sprinted forward, and Pickaxe and Nugget catapulted him downfield, hurling him up toward the roof. Nitro reared back and hit him with a cannon of a pass, the long bomb barreling in with meteoric speed. Hitting TNT right in his outstretched gloves, the ball blasted him into a blue whirl, the flashy completion sending all the Miners fans into whoops and roars.

It was a full five minutes before the announcer was able to speak over the crowd's noise. "And coaching the Taiko Colony Miners . . . Holy frakkin' heck, this is huge. Officially announcing his retirement from the game of Ultraball, I give you the Miners' coach: Strike Sazaki."

A spotlight trained on a lone figure in a blue jumpsuit walking up the stairs to his team's coach's box, his hood pulled low over his eyes.

Strike had been mentally preparing for this moment all week, but his world still began to crumble. His teeth gritted, his chin quivering, he tried in vain to fight back the tears.

ULTRABOWL XI

Neutron Nation was out in full force, on their feet, swearing, stomping, and screaming at a deafening pitch. Strike could barely hear himself think, much less make out what his players were saying through his headset. With helmet comms unreliable due to the earsplitting noise, his Miners would have to rely on hand signals and reading each other's lips during huddles.

Every cell in his body screamed at Strike to leap out on the field and demand his number 8 Ultrabot suit back. It was pure agony to no longer be one of the ten machines of war battling it out in the arena. But there was no doubt that he had made the right decision. Rock had even admitted he had suspected Strike's secret all along, having compiled a list titled "Evidence That Strike Might Be Outgrowing His Ultrabot Suit."

There was nothing Strike could do now except sit back and watch, hoping that he had done everything he possibly could to prepare his team for this do-or-die game. Strike prayed that the team's intense week of practice with the new lineup would pay off, and that Fusion's drills had set in for good. Nitro had been carrying an Ultraball cradled away in her arm every moment she was suited up, the other Miners trying to knock it out at any opportunity. After hundreds of hours of learning and drilling to protect the ball, today would be her ultimate test.

As the pregame players' meeting took place on the field, Strike looked nervously to the domed ceiling of the massive cavern, where all eight teams' logos had been etched for today's big game, and then to the luxury boxes high in the stands, where Zuna was sure to be sitting. He had already used a deadly weapon from a similar spot last year. If it looked like his Neutrons might lose, what would Zuna do this time to stop the Miners? Strike forced his gaze back to the field, but he couldn't shake the knowledge that Zuna would go to any length to win the massive bets he had placed upon his Neutrons.

Strike jolted back to the game when a chorus of boos erupted through the crowd. The small pocket of Miners fans dotted around the stands were chanting Nitro's name as the girl in the blue number 8 Ultrabot suit caught the opening kickoff.

"Torch!" she screamed into the helmet comm.

What with the stadium noise, it took a moment for Strike to figure out what Nitro had said. Then he grinned. Maybe Nitro had finally forgiven Torch. As if she didn't have enough motivation to win this game, doing it for her brother was going to fire her up even more.

Nitro juked a fast-approaching Neutron hard, making him fall over. She grabbed another defender's arm and threw him toward one of Saladin Stadium's all-new magnetic tornado zones. The Neutron bounced off the turf and then drove his boots into the ground, struggling in a desperate attempt to escape the zone's pull. But it yanked him backward off his feet and sucked him into its center. Accelerating quickly, the Neutron slammed into the turf at the center of the tornado zone, locked out of the rest of the play by an invisible force field.

In the meantime, Nitro had taken off running, the steel Ultraball safely tucked under her arm. She hurdled over another Neutron who had punched through the wedge of Miners blocking for her. She cut toward another tornado zone in the middle of the field. A Neutron defender had the angle on her and came in hot, flinging himself at her. But at the last second, Nitro cut back and leapt high into the air, throwing herself forward into a spin, just clearing the edge of the tornado zone. The incoming defender still managed to crack a fist into her, but she grabbed his glove and flung him toward the tornado zone. His eyes widened as he strained against the pull, his limbs wildly flailing as he got sucked into the electromagnetic black hole.

One last Neutron threw himself at Nitro, but she lowered her shoulder, curling both arms around the Ultraball. The Neutron slammed into her like a cannonball, both of them rolling toward the end zone. Although her arms were busy protecting the Ultraball, she bull-rushed her way across the goal line with the defender hanging all over her.

She thundered out a victorious bellow before rearing her arm back and hurling the Ultraball skyward. The missile of a throw sliced through the air and cracked into the exact center of the Neutrons' logo etched into the high ceiling, sending down a mist of gray moon dust. "No such thing as a curse!" she yelled, jabbing a finger toward the roof. "This one's for Torch!"

The rest of the Miners came in, chest-bumping and turbo butt-slapping Nitro. "Torch!" they screamed back.

The boos and swearing came raining down out of the Neutron Nation fans, Nitro's throw riling them up. But the contingent of Miners fans around Strike went wild, eating up her show of bravado. A radiant glow filled Strike's chest. After just twenty seconds, the Miners were up 7–0, and Nitro was on fire. Strike pumped a fist, saying a silent word of thanks to Fusion. The former quarterback's fumble drills had cured Nitro of her one glaring problem spot, turning her into a true superstar who would lead them to a title.

Then sharp pangs of guilt stabbed at Strike, his stomach churning. Nightmare images filled his head, of Fusion rotting away in jail, maybe even being tortured. There was nothing Strike could do about it right now. But winning this game would mean that Zuna would lose his fortune, and thus his power. Maybe then Strike could figure out a way to free Fusion.

There was no doubt that the Neutrons were talented, well deserving of the first seed in the playoffs. During the first half, White Lightning scored two rushing touchdowns and threw for two more. He danced around the edges of the tornado zones, elbowing Miners into them, once even knocking both Nugget and Pickaxe into a tornado zone one after the other. Defensively, he almost single-handedly broke up two touchdown passes, when he read the Miners' plays perfectly. If it hadn't been for Nitro's incredible accuracy, hitting TNT on full-field passes that locked right into the tips of his gloves, White Lightning would have had pick-sevens both times.

But White Lightning also took a few too many chances, slinging one pass to what looked like a wide-open Meltdown streaking toward the end zone, only to have TNT outleap Meltdown and return it for a touchdown. White

Lightning also fumbled once when Nitro tackled him, throwing both of them into a tornado zone, her fist slamming into his arm as they whipped into the eye of the hurricane. The costly turnover allowed the Miners to pull ahead to a 49–35 lead.

With a minute to go in the first half, the Neutrons had the ball at the Miners' forty-meter line, fourth down and a long way to go. If the Miners could stop the Neutrons on this play, they could simply run out the clock and go into halftime with a fourteen-point lead. Or the Miners could then take a shot for another touchdown. Strike rubbed his hands together, knowing exactly what he'd do if the Miners got the ball back: he'd stick the dagger into the heart of Neutron Nation, with a highball bounce off a slingshot V. The entire game, Nitro had thrown with uncanny precision. Even with TNT ricocheting crazily off the high ceiling, she'd sling a perfect full-field pass to him, the Ultraball lasering right into his outstretched gloves. A twenty-one-point lead at halftime would be devastating.

As the Miners huddled up, Strike squinted. He threw on his headset, yelling, "Rock, concentrate on the play!" Just like earlier in the season, Rock wasn't paying attention to the huddle. He was staring at the bottom of the scoreboard, trying to figure out an encoded message that started with three dots, then three dashes, then three dots. Strike jumped up and down, waving his hands in the air, trying to catch Rock's attention, but his rocketback 2's gaze was laser-locked onto the scoreboard.

Luckily, TNT noticed what was going on as they broke the huddle. He smacked Rock's helmet, pointing to where he was supposed to go. Rock flinched, seeming to come out of a trance. He looked around as if he was surprised to see himself on the field. TNT yanked at Rock to get him into the right position.

But the Neutrons took full advantage of the Miners' confusion. White Lightning quick-hiked the ball before TNT and Rock could get into place. He took off scrambling to his left, two blockers clearing the way for him. Tucking in the ball, he headed toward the edge of a tornado zone.

Hot in pursuit, Nitro vaulted over Nugget's back, leaping clear over a surprised Neutron blocker. The other one wasn't as easily fooled, though, timing his jump to smash a shoulder into Nitro, slamming her backward.

White Lightning was still heading toward the tornado zone, but he had no blockers now. Pickaxe raced forward, gaining speed as he lowered his shoulder to deliver a crushing blow.

Strike cupped his hands to his mouth, screaming to Pickaxe that it was a fake. They had prepared for all the Neutrons' trick plays, and this one was easily countered— as long as the defender didn't over-pursue in hopes of making a killing tackle. But Pickaxe fell for it, leaving his feet in an attempt to spear White Lightning in the middle of his chest plate.

White Lightning slid to the ground, ducking under Pickaxe's outstretched arms before catching one of Pickaxe's gloves to heave him straight into the tornado zone. Pickaxe roared as the electromagnetic forces sucked him in and slammed him to the ground. A split second later, White Lightning popped up and reversed course, scurrying along the edge of the zone. He cocked back the Ultraball as he ran, looking for Meltdown, who was streaking down the other sideline.

The Miners had one chance to break up this play. If Rock could rush at White Lightning fast enough and time his jump just right, he could force White Lightning into a tough pass. Rock might even bat down the Ultraball if he was lucky.

But Rock still seemed disoriented. He jumped at White Lightning well after the Neutrons' quarterback released the ball. Rock's outstretched arms weren't anywhere close enough to affect the throw.

Strike groaned, dropping his head into his hands. White Lightning's pass wasn't perfect, but Meltdown was a great rocketback. Strike had seen Meltdown make much harder catches than this. The entire stadium seemed to belong to Neutron Nation, a tremendous roar going up in anticipation of the big touchdown catch.

Suddenly, a collective gasp went up through the stands. Nitro had slung TNT high and hard, the Miners' rocketback 1 soaring in toward Meltdown. Just as Meltdown made an amazing one-handed grab, TNT cracked in with a wild barrage of punches and kicks.

A swarm of other players charged toward the spot where Meltdown and TNT were coming down, near the back right corner of the end zone. Meltdown was still trying to secure his grip on the ball when TNT landed a huge roundhouse punch, knocking it loose.

All eight other players jumped for it at the same time, a tangle of blue and red limbs mixed up, flailing, kicking, swatting at each other as they jockeyed for position. Time after time, the ball snapped into someone's glove electromagnet, only to be jarred loose by a punch or a swat. As the Ultraball fell and bounced off the turf, everyone dove for it, forming a writhing pileup near the goal line.

Three armored refs came running in, whistles blowing. One by one, they pulled players off the scrum, a Miner first, then a Neutron, then back and forth. Groans went up through the stands when the refs pulled away the last player, revealing that Rock had the ball. A ref signaled that the Miners had recovered, and a chorus of boos erupted through the stands.

As Rock got to his feet, Ion Storm, the Neutron's crackback 2, got right in his face. He flipped his visor to clear and shouted something at Rock that froze him in place for several seconds. A whistle blew to signify the end of the first half, but Rock still didn't move.

Strike jumped to his feet in alarm. Even with the Ultrabot suit on, Rock's body language was crystal clear. Whatever Ion Storm had said to him had badly shaken him. Strike tried to yell to Rock over the helmet comm, to tell him to not let the Neutrons get in his head, but he wasn't sure if Rock could hear him over the background roar of the crowd.

Then Rock popped to his feet and sprinted in a frenzy toward the locker rooms, well ahead of the other Miners. His helmet was in the process of rotating back over his head when Strike caught sight of his panicked face.

Something was wrong. Very wrong.

Strike tore down the steps toward the tunnel entrance leading into their locker room. He leaned over the railing, screaming at Rock as he passed by. "What is it? What's the matter?"

Rock barely paused as he sprinted by. "Dot dot dot, dash dash dash, dot dot dot," he shouted.

"You're not making sense. What does that—"

"Boom's life is in danger!"

MAKING THE CALL

BY THE TIME Strike had run down the length of the tunnel to the locker room, Rock was already out of his Ultrabot suit. Instead of neatly lining it up against the far wall like usual, it looked as if Rock had run right out of it, leaving the monstrous exoskeleton bent over into a crouch, its panels haphazardly flopped open. Rock was scratching madly onto a page of his notebook, so hard that he kept puncturing it. In ten years of being close friends, Strike had never seen Rock as frenzied.

All the Miners hovered over Rock's shoulder, trying to see what Rock was doing. "SOS?" Strike said in alarm. "Boom sent you an SOS message?"

"I figured out the first three letters in my head," Rock

said. "That worried me enough. And then what Ion Storm said to me after the last play . . ." He slammed a fist into a wall before working on the rest of the message.

"What did he say?" Strike asked.

Rock mumbled to himself, stuck in a trance as he continued decoding the message. The rest of the Miners surrounded him, looking over his shoulder as Rock scrawled away.

Strike glanced at the clock on the wall of the locker room—just twenty-five minutes until halftime ended. Boom's message might be important, containing critical information that would help the Miners win. But even though their surprise lineup had helped them build a lead, they still had a ton of work to do. The Neutrons were sure to make serious adjustments for the second half. Strike needed Rock's help to outthink Zuna. "Hey," he said as he placed a hand on Rock's shoulder. "Second half. I'm thinking have Nitro run the rocket booster option more. And mix it up, with TNT in on some of the dual quarterback sets we practiced. What do you think?"

"Uh-huh," Rock said. His focus was laser-locked onto his notebook.

Strike hesitated, but made a move to close up Rock's notebook. With so little time left to prepare, someone had to take charge and organize the Miners.

Rock slapped Strike's hand away in an uncharacteristic display of rage. "Stop," he said. "I'm almost done."

"We have to figure out what adjustments to make," Strike said. "I need a game plan. I have to—"

"Say goodbye to your girlfriend," Rock said.

"What?" Strike asked.

"That's what Ion Storm told me," Rock said. "Say goodbye to your girlfriend. All the Dark Siders will be dead in thirty minutes."

Strike looked at the other Miners. Everyone gaped at each other as they processed the message. Strike shook his head, trying to snap out of his shock. "Maybe that was just Ion Storm running his mouth," he said. "Trying to get inside your head."

Rock shot up off the bench, spinning around to hold up his notebook. It read:

SOS IN MORTAL DANGER BOOM

"Mortal danger?" Strike said. "No. Zuna couldn't have found her. Wraith said she's hidden away. Safe."

But if anyone could figure out a way to locate Boom and kill her, it's Zuna, he thought.

Then it hit him. His eyes going wide, he grabbed Rock's shoulders. "The Deathstrike Device," he said.

"We can talk more about that later," Rock said, shaking Strike off. "Right now, I need to figure out what this mortal danger is."

"The Deathstrike Device *is* the mortal danger."

Rock's forehead creased, his lips pinching into a tight line. "That's not possible. Didn't Chain Reaction say that Zuna needs to win his big bets on the Ultrabowl in order to have enough money to build the Deathstrike Device?"

"I don't know!" Strike shook Rock hard, willing him to listen. "Somehow, Zuna's already built the Deathstrike Device. Maybe it's just the first of many Deathstrike Devices. In just thirty minutes . . ."

In just thirty minutes, Raiden Zuna is going to wipe out all ten thousand people on the Dark Side of the moon, he thought.

"Call Boom," Strike said.

"Really?" Rock tilted his head. "I thought you said I should never use the phone she gave me, unless it was an absolute—"

"This is an absolute emergency!"

Rock nodded. "You're right." He stuck his hand in his jumpsuit pocket and fished out the phone Boom had given him at the end of last season. He looked to Strike, still uncertain.

The threat Ion Storm had issued to Rock loomed large in Strike's head. The Dark Siders were in mortal danger. "Make the call," he said.

His fingers flying, Rock punched in the secret code Boom had given him last year. Static appeared on the screen, and for a long moment, nothing happened.

Then Boom appeared. She squinted, her face gaunt and pale. "Rock?" she asked.

"Boom," Rock said. Although his face was still creased with tension, he smiled. "It's been so long since I've seen you." His eyes opened wide as he snapped out of his euphoria. "You're in mortal danger?"

"I am?" Boom asked. "What do you mean?"

Rock glanced at Strike, confusion wrinkling his brow. "The scoreboard message," Rock said. "Mortal danger."

"What are you talking about?" Boom said. "And why haven't you used any of the plays I've sent? A fourteen-point lead on the Neutrons is pretty good, but you could easily have been up twenty-eight if you had run TNT and Nitro on the alternating rocket booster option."

"B-b-but . . ." Rock stuttered. "You have been sending us messages through the scoreboards, right?"

"Yes." She lowered her head, averting her eyes. "After what happened last year, I owed it to the Miners to do anything I could to help deliver an Ultrabowl title. Especially considering how much money Zuna has bet on the Neutrons to win it all. You guys have to beat them. Run TNT and Nitro in the alternating rocket booster option. And swarm blitz White Lightning more, cornering him near the tornado zones. He's starting to play tired."

Rock and Strike stared at each other, dumbfounded. "But you sent an SOS," Rock said.

"No, I didn't. You really didn't decode the plays I sent you at the start of the game?"

Rock shook his head. "I don't get it. If you didn't send

the SOS, then who did?"

"And what about what Ion Storm said?" Strike added. "'Say goodbye to your girlfriend. All the Dark Siders will be dead in thirty minutes.'"

Rock blushed, turning deep red.

Boom rolled her eyes. She was about to say something when someone in a white jumpsuit tapped her on the shoulder. Her eyes narrowed as she leaned over to listen. "Movement? What kind of movement?" She nodded as the person kept whispering. After a few seconds, she turned to Rock. "Something's happening up on the surface of the moon. Something just launched."

A horrible dread seeped into Strike's bones. Chain Reaction's cryptic messages were finally starting to make sense. He grabbed Rock's shoulder, squeezing hard. "It's the Deathstrike Device," he said, his voice hollow.

Boom squinted at Strike. "What are you talking—"

"Zuna's going to murder everyone on the Dark Side," Strike yelled. "You have to get up to the surface of the moon to stop it."

"We can't get onto the surface of the moon. What are we supposed to do, waltz out the Dark Side airlock and hold our breath? Or how about we have a nice space picnic outside Moon Dock airlock?"

"You could get to the surface, if you were wearing an Ultrabot suit," Rock said. "They're essentially space suits, with self-contained oxygen generation."

Boom stared at him, her eyebrows scrunching together. "Yeah, okay. But how would I get—"

Rock spluttered, coughing. Jumping off the bench, he spit out his words in a panic. "Moon Dock airlock! The door isn't dusty because someone's been using it."

Strike and Rock stared at each other as the horrible truth materialized. "White Lightning," Strike said. "Fusion said that White Lightning has been building some big weapon for Zuna. Sneaking out at night."

"He's been taking weapon components up to the surface of the moon, while in his Ultrabot suit," Rock said. "The footprints reportedly seen in the Tunnel Ring late at night—they must have been White Lightning's."

Boom slowly processed everything, her jaw hanging low. "The thing that just launched. It *is* a weapon."

"But where would Zuna have gotten all the nuclear components?" Rock asked.

"All those nuclear parts that have gone missing from North Pole Colony," Boom said. "The thefts that Zuna's been blaming on me. He must have stolen them himself."

"And given them to White Lightning," Strike said. "So he can assemble them into the Deathstrike Device."

"And now it's on its way to kill you," Rock said in despair. "You have to evacuate—now."

"But wait," Strike said. "How could Zuna possibly know where Boom is? The Dark Side is an enormous place, half the entire moon . . ." He trailed off, the blood draining out of his face.

Boom finished his thought. "That thing up there launched shortly after you made this phone call. Zuna somehow used this very call to locate our position."

"Oh no," Strike said, a horrible dread churning his gut. "I was the one who made this possible. I told Rock to call you."

"Zuna tricked me," Rock said. "He somehow planted a fake message on the scoreboard. But how did he know? Did he notice me staring too hard at a scoreboard earlier in the season?" He swore under his breath. "That souvenir ball I accidentally drew the code on, after the Explorers game. Maybe Zuna got hold of it." He swore again and clapped his palms to his head. "I'm such an idiot. This was the only message that didn't start with *B-O-O-M*. I should have known it was a fake. You have to run. Get out of there. You might only have minutes left."

"That's impossible," Boom said, shaking her head. "It'd take hours to evacuate so many people."

"You have to try," Rock said. "There has to be a way."

"Can't be done."

"Maybe if—"

Boom whacked a button on the console in front of her. An image appeared on a giant screen behind her. It detailed a maze of underground passageways zigzagging everywhere, access codes displayed in tiny lettering. "See for yourself, genius. There's no frakkin' way."

Rock was quiet for a long moment as he studied the map, his eyes furiously flicking back and forth. "You're right," he finally said. "It's impossible."

Boom clenched her jaw. "Forget about me. Go beat the Neutrons. Raiden Zuna must not win his Ultrabowl bets. With that much money, he'll be unstoppable. He'll take over the entire moon." She squeezed her eyes tight. "This is all my fault. Sending secret messages through the scoreboards was a huge mistake." Turning away, her voice cracked. "I was so sure I'd see you again one day. Goodbye, Rock." The image blinked out.

Strike reeled, still trying to grasp it all. Could it really be possible that Raiden Zuna had pulled off such a devious plan? It was so complicated. Zuna had read and decoded the secret scoreboard messages that Boom had been sending? Then he had planted a fake one, tricking them into contacting Boom, thus giving away her position?

It seemed impossible. But Fusion had said that Zuna had ways of stealing other teams' signals—maybe he *had* intercepted Boom's messages.

And White Lightning would have had to spend a hundred hours carrying parts for the Deathstrike Device up to the surface of the moon—parts that Raiden Zuna had himself stolen from North Pole Colony.

Deep in his gut, Strike knew that's exactly what had happened. The only people that had the code for Moon

Dock airlock were the twenty-one colony governors. Zuna was one of them.

No wonder Zuna replaced Fusion with White Lightning, he thought. After his total humiliation during the one-on-one play with Boom last year, White Lightning had been desperate for a chance at survival. Desperate enough to do whatever Zuna ordered him to do.

And now the Deathstrike Device was on its way to murder the Dark Siders.

TNT pointed to the clock. "Second half starts in fifteen minutes." He glanced at Rock uneasily. "You heard Boom. We have to stop Zuna from winning all the bets he placed on his Neutrons." He leaned in toward Strike, pleading. "There is nothing more important than winning this game. We can't do anything to help the Dark Siders, anyway."

"Wait," Strike said. A crazy notion swirled inside his head. "Maybe we can." He looked over to their Ultrabot suits, lined up against the wall. "We could get up to the surface of the moon. In our suits. That map Boom brought up. One of those tunnels must lead to that Dark Side airlock she mentioned. Right, Rock? Did you record the call?"

The locker room went quiet. No one moved, except for Rock nodding in a daze. He raised the phone, scrolling through the recording until he found the giant map of the Dark Siders' tunnels.

Then TNT exploded. "You want us to leave the game? No frakkin' way. We'd forfeit. You heard Boom. She told us that we had to go defeat the Neutrons. Plus, who knows if that thing up there is a weapon or not? Maybe it's just a communications satellite or something."

"The nuclear spear that Zuna used to nuke Chain Reaction," Strike said. Chain Reaction's cryptic statements and the way he had raised his arms toward the ceiling—it was all making sense now. "The Deathstrike Device is an enormous version of that." If that was the case, its focused beam might be able to shoot lethal radiation through tons of moon rock, nuking the Dark Siders to hell.

Rock grabbed the front of Strike's jumpsuit with one hand, holding up his phone with the other. "There's a hidden passageway to the Dark Side airlock, accessible through the Tunnel Ring. We can get to the surface. We have to go. Now."

"Whoa, whoa," TNT said. "Even if it is a weapon, we couldn't stop it. Can't you see how stupid it would be to abandon this game? We can't forfeit." He swallowed hard. "Please, Strike. We have to win this game."

Strike's gaze bounced back and forth between his two players, the opposing views smashing into each other. What if he led his Miners up to the surface of the moon, only to see something harmless, like TNT had said? The Miners would be a laughingstock, the butt of jokes everywhere. The Underground Ultraball League might even take away the franchise for forfeiting the Ultrabowl.

And there was the issue of Raiden Zuna betting his entire fortune on his Neutrons winning the Ultrabowl. No one but the Miners stood in the Neutrons' way now.

A buzzer sounded through the stadium, echoing down the tunnel and into the locker room. All eyes were trained on Strike, waiting for him to make the biggest decision of his life. Whatever he decided, it might lead to Raiden Zuna taking over the moon. The fate of thousands of people rested upon his shoulders.

Gathering his resolve, Strike straightened his jumpsuit, hoping against hope that he hadn't just doomed them all. "Everyone get suited up," he said.

HAIL MARY

STRIKE CLUNG TO the back of TNT's Ultrabot suit, a mere speck of a boy on the back of the giant robot, as the Miners raced through the secret tunnels. His arms were shaking uncontrollably, ghostly images flaring in the blackest corners of his mind. The emergency lights on the Ultrabot suits barely held back the darkness, casting terrifying red shadows that leapt at Strike as the Miners tore through the turns.

At this breakneck speed, Strike might die if he slipped and fell, slamming to the ground with no protection. But he willed TNT to run even faster. He prayed that they'd see nothing above the moon except a harmless satellite, even though that would mean facing severe penalties from the Underground Ultraball League for forfeiting this playoff game.

Charging along behind Rock's lead, the Miners soon arrived at the Dark Siders' airlock door leading to the surface of the moon. Rock skidded to a halt by the control panel, studying it intently.

"We still have time to get back to the game," TNT said.

"We have to do this," Strike replied through his headset. "You know that."

"No, I don't. We're making a huge mistake."

Following Rock's instructions, Strike carefully punched in a series of buttons on the control panel, the sequence of numbers Rock had seen on Boom's map. With a low rumbling of gears and motors, the door slid open, revealing two airlocks.

Rock pointed to a small room on the other side of one of the airlocks. "I think that's an observation chamber," he said. "Strike should be able to see what's going on from there."

"You should go up to the surface instead of me, Strike," Pickaxe said. "Take my Ultrabot suit."

"No time," Strike said. "I'll watch from inside the observation chamber. Everyone else, go."

"Strike," TNT said. "We have to return to the game—"

"No!" Strike pressed two buttons, starting the process of cycling both airlocks. "I order you to get up there."

TNT held his ground, looking back the way they came, his jaw set in determination. "You can't make me."

Strike bit his lip. "You're right. I can't force you to do this. But I'm asking you. I'm begging you. As one of your closest friends. Thousands of lives are at stake." He pointed to the airlock leading out to the surface of the moon. "Please."

After a pause, TNT nodded, joining the others.

Strike's airlock door closed behind him, pumps and motors whirring as the system cycled. Two minutes later, a green light flashed, and he quickly scrambled through the far door into the small observation chamber.

Strike sucked in a sharp breath, his brain unable to process the sight in front of him. He had heard so many stories about the horrors of outer space, the deathly blackness that the Moon Dock airlock door kept at bay. But no one had prepared him for the dazzling glory of a billion stars. The epic panorama of shimmering lights stunned him, freezing his feet to the floor. Dizziness washed over him, a mix of amazement and sheer panic, that only a clear window separated him from the unparalleled majesty of outer space. He nearly fell backward, stumbling as he plopped down onto a bench. Something this beautiful was impossible.

Strike sat in awe until a shout came into his headset. "Airlock's done," Rock said. "We're heading up to the surface."

Banks of monitors lined the observation room, cameras giving Strike a remote view of the five suited-up Miners racing up the tunnels. They zigzagged through curving switchbacks as they made their way to the surface of the moon.

Strike leaned in to study the bank of monitors, focusing in on a camera that was aimed into space. A bolt of panic shot through him. He worked the controls to zoom in on something floating above the surface of the moon. Glowing with an orange hue, lights flashed down the entire length of the giant machine. "It's just like the thing Chain Reaction described—the nuclear spear that Zuna used to nuke him," he said. "Only a whole lot bigger."

The five Miners emerged onto the surface of the moon, finally coming into Strike's direct view through the panoramic window. In shock, TNT jabbed a finger toward the giant weapon. "You were right," he said. "That's no ordinary satellite."

Rock slammed his fists against his helmet. "It's too far away to leap at, even inside an Ultrabot suit." He swiveled to Nitro and grabbed her shoulders. "Throw me at it. Heave me with everything you've got."

"No," Strike said, the hairs on the back of his neck prickling. "There'd be no way to get back to the surface of the moon. You'd float off into outer space and die."

"Doesn't matter," Rock said. "This is all my fault. I have to do this."

"Even with a slingshot V, you wouldn't get there," TNT said. "It's too far off."

"We have to do something," Rock said.

Everyone went silent. Strike could only watch as the Deathstrike Device floated through space away from them. Waves of sickening nausea crashed through his chest, drowning him. Leading his Miners up to the surface of the moon had been the worst mistake of his entire life. Like TNT had said, this was all for naught. He had done nothing to save the Dark Siders. Worse yet, by abandoning the Ultrabowl against the Neutrons, he had cleared the way for Raiden Zuna to take over the entire moon. When Zuna won his bets on the Ultrabowl, he'd make an arsenal of weapons like this one.

They were too late. There was no way to stop the Deathstrike Device. It was so far away that they'd need a slingshot zone to reach it. Or one of the Farajah Flame-throwers' arm cannons.

Arm cannons . . .

An idea came to him. It wasn't a good one. But they had no other options. "Nitro," he said. "Are you carrying your Ultraball?"

"Now isn't the time to be thinking about Ultraball," Rock said. "We have to—"

"Nitro!" Strike shouted. "Did you bring it or not?"

She turned toward the observation chamber window in confusion. Slowly, she raised the Ultraball she always carried around with her. "Yeah. Just like Fusion told me to. Why—"

"You can hit the Deathstrike Device," Strike said. "It's far away. But you can make this throw."

Nitro stepped backward, shaking her head. "No way. I can't make that shot. You have to come up and do it, Strike. I'm heading back to the airlock so you can suit up."

"You can do it," Strike said. "You're the best person for this. Even if we did have time for me to get into a suit, I'd still pick you to make the throw. You hit the Neutrons' logo, dead center in the high ceiling. And remember that pass you lasered into TNT's outstretched gloves on the third play of the game today?"

"I was shooting like a frakkin' missile off the slingshot V," TNT said. "You hit me right on the dot. Not even a centimeter off."

"But this is different," Nitro said. "If I miss, people will die. I can't do it."

Rock grabbed her shoulders. "You have to make the throw—now. Every second, the Deathstrike Device is moving farther away. Do it. Now."

"Please, Nitro," Strike said. "You have the best arm in the league. You have to do it."

She shook her head, trembling with fear.

"Magnetize the ball," Strike shouted.

The Miners all turned to look back at the observation chamber, silent in their confusion.

"Nitro, give Rock the Ultraball so he can magnetize it," Strike said, his words rushing out. "That way, you'll only have to get close with your throw. It'll be easy."

"What?" Rock asked. "But—"

"Rock," Strike shouted. "Magnetize. The. Ultraball. Like that list in your notebook. About all the ways of making hardtack bars taste better? Remember the title of that list?"

His brow wrinkled, Rock thought for a long moment. Then he held his hand out to Nitro. "Give it to me."

Nitro looked up, flipping her helmet visor to clear. "You can really magnetize an Ultraball? How?"

Rock snatched the heavy steel ball from her and snaked his gloved hands across the ball's length, stroking it slowly, carefully, from nose to nose. He repeated this five times. "Done," he said. He held it back out to Nitro.

She took it in her gloved hands, hefting its weight. Raising it to eye level, she squinted. "Doesn't seem any different."

"Just get it close and it'll lock on," Strike said through his headset. "You got this. You're Nitro."

After a long pause, she nodded.

Strike sat forward in his seat. With every moment she delayed, the throw would get more difficult. But Nitro didn't move. Each second that ticked away became more excruciating. *Why doesn't she just let it fly?* Strike thought in aggravation.

And then it hit him: everyone was staring at her. The pressure had paralyzed her. "Pickaxe," he shouted into his headset. "Atomic wave blitz, stunt red."

"What?" Pickaxe said. "Why the frak would we rush her?"

Strike took a deep breath. "Miners, I need you all to listen to me and follow my game plan," he said, his voice commanding. "Game time. Atomic wave blitz, stunt red. Do it."

Pickaxe turned to look at Strike through the observation window. He nodded and raced off a few steps. He got into a three-point stance, his right glove in a fist touching the ground. "I'm charging in at you in three seconds. Nugget, too." He waved his brother over.

"What are you doing?" TNT said. "Just leave her alone and let her make the frakkin' throw."

Nugget ran over, joining his brother. "We're coming after you, Nitro."

"I'm taking you down," Pickaxe said. "You can't make this play, you little girly."

Nitro's face hardened, her eyes slitting down. "What did you just say?"

"You throw like a girl," Pickaxe said. "That puny girl arm can't get a throw past the mighty Pickaxe. I'm gonna frakkin' bury you." He snapped his head up, growling.

"TNT and Rock, line it up," Nitro said. "Let's show these frakkin' big mouths how it's done."

"I didn't say anything," Nugget squeaked.

Pickaxe shushed his brother and shoved him into a three-point stance by his side.

Nitro put the Ultraball on the ground, holding it with one hand as TNT and Rock lined up on either side of her. "Fly fifty-four," she yelled. "On two. Hut hut!"

As she picked up the ball and backpedaled, Pickaxe and Nugget came blitzing in with full heads of steam. TNT and Rock smashed into the brothers, but each of them rolled around the outside and then charged in toward Nitro.

She stepped forward in the pocket and reared her arm back before heaving the Ultraball at the Deathstrike Device. It flashed through the blackness of space, a silver blur blasting into the stars.

As soon as she let it go, she turned to Pickaxe, who was coming in hot. Lowering her shoulder, she crashed into his chest plate. She wrapped him up with both arms and pile-drove him into the surface of the moon. "Don't ever call me a little girly again!" she shouted.

His helmet smashed into the ground, Pickaxe grumbled. "I was just trying to motivate you."

"Oh," Nitro said. "Gotcha. Sorry." She picked him up and put him back on his feet.

Rock pointed at the Ultraball, streaking like a comet toward the Deathstrike Device. "It's on target," he said.

Strike pressed into the observation window, locked

onto Nitro's throw. The chatter on helmet comm went deathly quiet as the Ultraball closed in. At first, Strike thought it was right on course, but now, he dug his fingernails into his legs.

The throw was soaring high.

Strike got to his feet, pressing his face against the observation window. Bending backward, he willed the ball to pull down just a hair.

The five Miners on the moon's surface stared, watching the ball soar. "It might go high," Nitro said. "Good thing it's magnetized."

"Uh," Rock said into the helmet comm. "About that."

"Not now," Strike said into his headset. "Wait until—"

"I didn't really magnetize the ball," Rock said. "That's impossible, as impossible as making a hardtack bar taste good. Strike just needed to trick you into making the throw."

"What?" Nitro shouted. "I'm going to kill you both!"

"Quiet," Strike said. For a horrible moment, it looked like the Ultraball would sail over the giant spear-shaped object. But it cracked into the top of the spear, the heavy steel ball smashing a hole straight through its target, a spray of electronic shrapnel bursting out the other side.

No one said a word as the weapon tilted off-kilter. Going into a slow spin, the Deathstrike Device continued to glow with its orange aura.

Strike's eyes widened in horror. Had they actually

made things worse? What if they had just made the weapon shoot an intense beam of focused nuclear radiation all over the moon? Nightmares clawed into his head.

I might have just wiped the entire human race off the face of the moon.

But then a storm of white sparks burst out of the Deathstrike Device. Orange and red crackles of electricity arced down the length of the giant spear. Strike flung himself away from the window as a blinding flash lit his retinas into firestorms of agony. A moment later, he was thrown off his feet, slamming into the back wall of the observation chamber.

His head spinning, his ears pounding, Strike tried to stand up. He immediately collapsed back to the ground. Pressing his hands against the sides of his head, he felt something sticky. An ooze of red covered his fingers.

Still woozy, Strike blinked furiously through the burst of intense light still imprinted on the backs of his eyes. A billowing cloud of gray smoke was expanding out from where the Deathstrike Device had been, furious eddies swirling through the angry mass, as if it were alive. The cloud of death billowed toward him.

Strike reached for his headset, which had been blown off when he had hit the wall, and pulled it back on. All five Miners were shouting over each other in a frenzied panic. Then he picked out Rock's voice, repeating himself in an impressively stoic fashion: "Everyone calm down and wait for your suits to finish rebooting," he kept on saying.

Strike looked out the big window, nearly choking at the sight of his Miners all lying on their backs on the surface of the moon. "Are you guys okay?" he screamed.

"The blast shorted out and reset all our suits," Rock said. "But we'll be fine, even if the cloud reaches us. You, on the other hand, need to get through your airlock. Now."

Strike ran for the airlock door, but a horrible thought stopped him in his tracks. "That cloud. Have we just killed everyone on the moon?"

"Only focused radiation can penetrate through tons of moon rock," Rock said. "The blast cloud is dispersed. Get back underground—far underground—and you'll be safe. Don't wait for us. Run."

"Okay," Strike said. "But get the frak out of there as soon as you can." Then he frantically pushed the airlock's activation button. The door slowly opened. It would take two minutes for the airlock to cycle. That was two minutes the dark cloud of deadly radiation would have to creep toward him, enveloping him in its toxic embrace.

The clear airlock door closed, oxygen hissing into the chamber. There was nothing Strike could do but wait, watching the countdown timer and the cloud in their deadly race. Strike pressed himself against the back wall, shoving himself into a corner, as far away from the lethal cloud as possible.

As the seconds ticked away, Strike's worries turned to

his Miners, still on the moon's surface. An Ultrabot suit was designed to protect its wearer from just about anything, at least for a while. But what if the suits never came back online? Dread built into an overwhelming panic as he imagined his closest friends pinned in place, imprisoned by their inactive suits. He closed his eyes, trying to banish the image of his Miners struggling in their armored prisons, slowly suffocating as their oxygen stores drained away.

Thankfully, TNT spoke. "I'm back online," he said.

"Almost there," Nugget said. "My power bar just flashed on."

"Me too," Pickaxe chimed in. "Let's get the frak out of here."

Strike watched through the giant window as all his Miners got to their feet in succession, everyone running back to the airlock.

Everyone except Rock.

TNT noticed first, racing back to Rock, who was still laid out on the ground. "Rock. Rock!" He motioned to the others in a frenzy. "Help me pick him up!"

Frantic voices blared through the helmet comm as the others realized what was going on. Nitro, Pickaxe, and Nugget ran back, getting in place to pick Rock up off the surface.

"Stop," Rock said over helmet comm. "I need to study

this." He shook everyone off and sat up, pointing to the cloud.

"Let's get out of here," Nitro said. She yanked at Rock's arm, but he batted her away and jabbed his finger at the cloud again.

"I recognize the blast pattern," Rock said. "I'm sure of it."

"Never mind it," Strike yelled. "Just get out of there."

"We have to get through the airlock," TNT said. "We can get Strike back underground and to safety a lot faster if he's riding on my—"

"The Fireball Blast," Rock said.

Despite his mounting panic at the approaching cloud of death, Strike froze. "What did you say?" he asked.

"This blast pattern," Rock said. "It's much bigger in scale, but the pattern matches every single piece of data I've studied about the Fireball Blast. Exactly. Could that mean . . ."

Strike's mouth went dry. His panic twisted, morphing, transforming into a furious rage. "Raiden Zuna was behind the Fireball Blast." He slammed a fist into a wall of the observation chamber. "I'll kill him! I'll—"

The airlock door behind him slid open. After another minute, the five Miners in Ultrabot suits met Strike on the other side of the chamber. All their visors were flipped to clear, and all of them were shouting at once.

Strike climbed up on TNT's back. Clinging on with all his might, Strike nearly fell off as TNT exploded into a sprint toward the door leading back into the Dark Siders' secret tunnels.

As they raced away, Strike made a vow. He didn't know how. He didn't know when. But at that moment, he swore to himself that he would get vengeance against Raiden Zuna.

The man who had killed his parents in the Fireball Blast ten years ago.

UNDERGROUND ULTRABALL LEAGUE: ULTRABOWL RESULTS

Year	Ultrabowl	Champions	Losing Team	MVP	Score
2343	I	Kamar Explorers	Saladin Shock	Berzerkatron	35-14
2344	II	Tranquility Beatdown	Farajah Flamethrowers	The Mad Mongol	49-28
2345	III	Saladin Shock	Tranquility Beatdown	Electrify	56-42
2346	IV	Farajah Flamethrowers	Kamar Explorers	Beastfire	70-63
2347	V	Farajah Flamethrowers	Tranquility Beatdown	Beastfire	63-56
2348	VI	Tranquility Beatdown	Farajah Flamethrowers	Genghis Brawn	77-70
2349	VII	North Pole Neutrons	Taiko Miners	Chain Reaction	70-56
2350	VIII	North Pole Neutrons	Taiko Miners	Chain Reaction	77-70
2351	IX	North Pole Neutrons	Taiko Miners	Chain Reaction	98-91
2352	X	North Pole Neutrons	Taiko Miners	Chain Reaction	DQ
2353	XI	North Pole Neutrons	Taiko Miners	Meltdown	DQ

The Lunar World News *Report*

SPACE EXPLOSION A HARMLESS NATURAL PHENOMENON

By Aziz Chang, Senior Grand High Executive Reporter

The giant "explosion" in space two days ago has been confirmed to be an enormous solar flare. An investigative team organized by *Lunar World News*, composed of experts from every different discipline, has given their conclusive report to the Council of Governors. "There is nothing to worry about," said Kaylen Lin, the captain of the Blackguard, who chaired the special commission. "Solar flares of this magnitude are rare, but they aren't harmful."

Meanwhile, the Underground Ultraball League has also closed their investigation into the Miners' Ultrabowl disqualification, the game pundits are now calling "The Strikeout Bowl." While the Miners have been fined, given a formal warning, and will lose their franchise upon the next infraction, that was the extent of their penalty. Considering how egregious their action was—depriving tens of thousands of fans of an entire half of Ultrabowl action—many are calling for a second investigation.

The Miners are officially the only team to have

been disqualified from an Ultrabowl—and twice in a row now. Raiden Zuna, owner of the five-time champion North Pole Neutrons, said, "The Miners are an embarrassment to the league. Taiko Colony has proven that it doesn't deserve an Ultraball team. Frankly, I'd like to see the Miners moved to Guoming Colony. Don't you think they'd look good in pink? 'The Guoming Junkers' has a nice ring to it."

Although Mr. Zuna may have been joking about a move to Guoming Colony, there is no doubt that the moon backs Mr. Zuna in a serious way. Polls taken after the Ultrabowl show his approval rating at a record 94 percent, over 40 percent higher than any other colony governor.

The Miners were contacted for this story, but Strike only continued to tell his far-fetched tale of a nuclear bomb in outer space. Beastfire, a leading Ultraball authority and MVP of Ultrabowls IV and V, said, "Of course Strike is gonna try to cover up the cowardly way he made his team retreat. Bunch of frakkin' crap he's spewing. What moron is gonna believe that the Miners went up into outer space? No one is that crazy. Truth is that Strike got scared. He's a gutless chicken. When the pressure is on, he crumbles. He couldn't take the thought of a fifth straight loss to the dynasty that is the North Pole Neutrons, so he threw the game in a way that would seem so ridiculous that people would have to believe him. But none of us do. We all see through you, Strike. He's a liar who's gonna git what's a-comin' to him. End of story."

Governor Katana of Taiko Colony, whose approval rating has plummeted to 13 percent, was not available for comment, as he is still under official investigation for potentially aiding and abetting the Miners in their egregious actions.

THE FIREBALL FIVE

A FEW DAYS later, all the Miners followed Strike up to an airlock door leading into Taiko Arena. "Okay, enough mystery," TNT said. "Just tell us why we're here, already."

"Nope," Strike said. He hit the entry button, and the door slid back with a hydraulic hiss.

Rock was the first one through the door. He stopped suddenly, the others bumping into him. "Is that . . ." He squinted. "Wraith?"

"And Smuggler and Cutter?" TNT added.

"Don't forget Big Bertha and Catacomb," Strike said, pointing to the two frail-looking crackbacks in gray jumpsuits. "The Cryptomare Molemen."

"What are you guys doing here?" Nugget said.

"I owe Wraith, big-time," Strike said. "She saved my life. Twice." He stuck out his hand. "I should never have doubted you. The rebellion. It's way more important than I ever imagined." Fiery tears started to burn his eyes. It had been three days now since Rock had made the connection between Zuna and the Fireball Blast that had killed so many people, including at least one parent of each of the Fireball Five. He took a deep breath, forcing himself to channel that anger, that fury, into a single-minded goal: to take down Raiden Zuna.

"Took you long enough to figure that out," Wraith said, a wry grin on her face.

"Have you heard from Boom?" Strike said. "Do you know if she's okay?"

Wraith's face fell. She shook her head, turning away. "They all went into hiding. I have to believe that they're fine. The rebellion has to rise." She cut her eyes to Strike. "So you're in?"

"I'm in," Strike said. "I don't know what I can do. But I'm all in."

"What you can do is lead us."

"You mean, like I led my team to our fifth straight Ultrabowl loss? To making it look like we threw the game?"

Wraith's face hardened. "You might not see it right now. But you are exactly what the rebellion needs. Who else would have made the call to leave the Ultrabowl and find a way to blow up the Deathstrike Device? You saved Boom's life. And a whole lot of others."

Deep down, Strike knew she had a point. But the sting of his Miners' fifth straight Ultrabowl loss—people all over the moon were calling Ultrabowl XI "The Strike-out Bowl"—was still raw. He was oozing despair, an overwhelming feeling of total failure blanketing his shoulders. "How are we going to stop someone as powerful as Zuna?" he asked. "Especially after winning his huge bet on the Ultrabowl? He has the entire moon thinking the explosion was a frakkin' solar flare."

"It's ridiculous," Wraith said.

"Yeah. But people are buying it. Eating it up. No one believes that we're crazy enough to go out an airlock." He shook his head. "With so many news reports confirming the solar flare story, giving so many details on what 'really happened,' even I'm starting to believe it a little."

"You and Boom will figure something out," Wraith said. "Together, the two of you are unstoppable. I have faith in you. We all do." She turned, all her Molemen nodding their heads with confidence. "Okay. Enough of this right now. Let's go play."

"Play?" Rock asked. "Play what?"

"Ultraball, of course," Wraith said. She turned to Strike. "I thought you said he's the smartest person you've ever known."

Strike grinned, nudging Rock. "There are a lot of

different types of smart," he said.

"There certainly are," Rock said. "I count twelve so far. Let me show you." He rifled through his notebook before Strike grabbed it and shoved it back into his pocket.

"Let's go," Wraith said. She waved to her teammates, who followed her toward the visiting team's locker room.

"You have your Ultrabot suits?" TNT said. "Here?"

"I said I owed Wraith, big-time," Strike said. "And she called in the favor."

"Losing to the Neutrons in the semis . . ." Wraith trailed off, her face tortured. "I'll never be able to forget that."

"It was my fault," Strike said. "I was the one who got you trapped in the junk hole. You wouldn't have gotten injured if it hadn't been for me."

"Forget about it," Wraith said. "Let's just see who would have won the real Ultrabowl. Even on your home field, we're gonna put you in a world of hurt."

"Big talk from a little girl," Pickaxe said. His eyes flashed wide open as he realized what he had said. "Uh. I didn't mean . . . uh . . ." He turned to his brother. "Help!"

Wraith's entire body tensed up, her fists trembling. She strode to Pickaxe, who held his ground at first. But as she approached, he backed up.

"I didn't mean it," Pickaxe squeaked. "It just slipped out." He held his hands in front of his face as Wraith leaned menacingly in. A little squeal escaped from his mouth.

Wraith broke into a chuckle and punched Pickaxe in the chest. She waved her team toward the locker room. "Come on, Molemen. Let's go suit up and then beat them down." They ran off in a tight formation, zigging and zagging, moving together like a machine. The five Molemen broke into a perfectly orchestrated roll, popping into a series of synchronized high-flying kicks and punches on their way to their locker room.

All the Miners turned to Pickaxe, who had flushed deep red. "Why'd you have to go and call her a little girl?" TNT said.

"Thanks a lot for making them angry, dummy," Nugget said.

"You're the dummy," Pickaxe grumbled.

Rock shook his head as he wrote in his little notebook. "This is going at the top of my list of 'Most Idiotic Things a Miner Has Ever Said.'" He held up his notebook. "Hey, look. Pickaxe now has the top three slots."

Nugget broke into laughter, cracking up so hard he farted. "Stop," he said through his uncontrollable giggles. "You're going to make me poop my pants."

"Okay, enough of that," Strike said. "Our Ultrabot suits—" He paused. "I mean, *your* Ultrabot suits, are waiting in the locker room." All the excitement, the anticipation, the awesomeness of this upcoming game drained right out of him. Even though it had been over a week now since he had stepped down as quarterback, the realization that his Ultraball career was over kept on slugging him in the gut. The raw hunger to play, to battle his way to the Ultrabowl title he had worked so hard for, felt as urgent as it had that horrible day when he had made his decision to hang it all up.

He closed his eyes, too tired to fight the pain. *Will I ever get past the end of my Ultraball career?* At age thirteen, he had already reached the peak of his life. Without Ultraball, he was a hollow shell. Empty inside.

"Uh . . . Strike?" TNT said. "Coach? You okay?"

Strike turned away, wiping his eyes. He wanted so badly to tell everyone that it was nothing. That they should head to the locker room and prepare for this once-in-a-lifetime opportunity. But all he could do was eke out a nod.

"It's probably not what you want to hear, but you're critical to the Miners as a coach," Rock said. "You're the one who decided to listen to my rants about Boom sending us secret messages. You're the one who put Nitro in at quarterback. You're our leader."

Strike started to protest again, but Nugget jumped in. "I love playing," he said. "But way more than that, I love playing for you. You're my coach, Strike. You always will be. Even after my Ultraball career ends, you'll still be my coach. For the rest of my life."

"Even if you're not playing, you're our leader," Pickaxe said. "I would follow you to the ends of the moon. I'd go into outer space for you. Frak, I *did* go into outer space for you. I'd die for you, Strike."

"We all would," TNT added. "There's a reason why Boom needs you to lead the rebellion."

"There's no one else on the moon who could," Rock said.

With everyone gazing at him, Strike had to choke back all the emotions welling up. For years, he had led the Taiko Miners as their quarterback, letting his play on the field speak for itself. Yes, he had been the coach, but in name only, leaving most of the analysis, strategy, and tactics up to Rock. Maybe if he worked hard enough at it, one day he could become a good coach. A great coach.

Maybe even lead his Miners to an Ultrabowl title.

He nodded, turning to wipe away the tears still stubbornly brimming over. A jumble of thoughts careened through his head, and he struggled to figure out what to say. But a glance over at their locker room started to bring everything into focus. "We have a lot of work to do for next year, both on and off the field. But for right now, we have a game to win. Let's go kick some Molemen butt."

As they approached the locker room, Strike looked up at the five Ultrabot suits lined neatly along the wall. Even after five years of playing, a sense of awe filled him every time he saw the suits. Although it was no longer his, he couldn't help but stroke the chest plate of the number 8 Ultrabot suit, its shiny blue paint chipped from the hits and collisions of the season, but the impactanium armor underneath completely intact.

"Ow," Nitro said. She leaned against a wall, holding her ankle, wincing with pain.

"You okay?" Strike asked. "What happened?"

"I twisted it. Tripped over my own feet. How frakkin' stupid. Guess you'll have to play quarterback out there."

"How did you trip over your own feet? You're the least klutzy person I know . . ." Strike trailed off. "You're not hurt. You're the best person to play quarterback. So suit up."

"No, really, I'm hurt," Nitro said. She rubbed her ankle. "Seriously. It's bad."

"You're the worst actor I've ever seen," Strike said. "You realize that even if you were really hurt, I'd play TNT at quarterback instead of me, right?"

Nitro shot TNT a meaningful look, raising an eyebrow.

"Ow," TNT said. "I hurt my . . . butt?"

Everyone burst out laughing.

"Enough jokes," Strike said. "Your ankle is fine, Nitro. And TNT's butt . . . Let's not go there. Now come on, it's game time."

"I'll always do whatever you say, Strike," Nitro said. "After this once. Today, you're going to play quarterback for the Taiko Miners."

"We're not going to take no for an answer," TNT said. "This one's yours, Strike. You've earned it."

"But—"

"Suit up one last time," Nitro said. "Do it already, before I change my mind."

Strike studied all the faces watching him, beaming at their leader. He took a long, hard look at the number 8 Ultrabot suit.

Pickaxe shoved him toward it. "Will you hurry up already? We got a game to play."

With a cautious step into one of the foot supports, Strike raised himself into place. Would the suit even seal up around him at this point? The chest plate slowly winched shut. The armor around his legs clicked together. Impactanium panels hinged closed around his arms. For a horrible moment, a warning light flashed onto the heads-up display inside the helmet lowering into place. But it was only a yellow light, only cautioning him of a tight fit. Strike relaxed his arms, trying to make them as small as possible, and the last armored panels clicked into place. His left shoulder was already pinching up, but he could manage it for one last game.

One last game. The prospect of living the rest of his life constantly looking backward, at his incredible days of playing Ultraball, had haunted him for weeks now. It was a gloomy specter filling all his nightmares. His teammates had granted him one more game, and he had to make it count.

He waited as his teammates suited up and got in

formation around him. He lifted a fist into the air. "Miners together," he said.

"Miners forever!" came the united cry from his teammates.

As Strike walked toward the door, he looked over at Nitro, hanging back by the lockers. It took an incredible person to give a gift like this. It was impossible to understand her sacrifice until you had experienced the pure joy of locking into an Ultrabot suit and transforming into a superhero. Giving up even a single game was something that hardly any Ultraball player would do.

"Go get 'em, Strike," Nitro said. "It might not be official, but when the Miners crush the Molemen out there, we'll know who the champs really are. Miners forever."

Nitro's words made Strike pause, filled with appreciation for how lucky he was. The Fireball Five had been his only real family for so long, but he had quickly grown to trust and depend upon Nitro. Although today would be the very last time he'd mount up inside an Ultrabot suit, maybe his future wouldn't be nearly as grim as it had seemed.

"Wait a minute," he said. "As the general manager and coach of the Miners, I've made a decision." He took a deep breath.

He started clicking out of his Ultrabot suit.

"What, you have to pee?" Pickaxe said with a chuckle. He halted, looking back toward the waste recyclers.

"Frak. Now I have to pee."

"I don't have to pee," Strike said. "I have to make way for the Miners' quarterback." He motioned to Nitro. "What are you waiting for? We don't have all day."

Nitro shook her head. "Play one last game, Strike. I want you to."

"I know, and I appreciate that," Strike said. "But as the coach and general manager of the Miners, it's my job to field the team that gives us the best chance of winning." He stepped down from the leg mounts and moved aside. "For that, I need you at quarterback. For today, for tomorrow, and for as long as you can still suit up."

"Are you sure?" Nitro said. "I mean, I would hate to give up even one game, but if you really don't want to play . . ."

"Will you just suit up already?" Strike said. A huge part of his brain was screaming at him to push Nitro aside and click back in. But he gritted his teeth, holding that urge at bay, as Nitro stepped into the leg mounts and sealed herself into place.

After her helmet locked down, Nitro's voice came onto Strike's headset. "Ready, Coach."

"Okay, QB," Strike said. "Give the Molemen no mercy. I'll be talking to you out there from the stands." He began the traditional Miners' cheer, but then backed off. He nodded to Nitro. "It's all you, QB."

"You sure?" Nitro asked.

"Lead out your team," Strike said. He paused. "Zuna took away your chance to win a big game for your brother. So go do it now. Win this one. For Torch."

The other Miners stared in silence at Nitro as she blinked hard, her eyes welling. "Thanks, Strike," she finally said. "You don't know how much that means to me."

"Actually, I think I do," Strike said. He glanced toward TNT and nodded.

TNT took a deep breath. "Thanks, Strike. For everything. I . . ." He choked up.

"Okay, okay," Pickaxe said. "Enough with the kissy-kissy stuff. Time to go smash up the Molemen. We still owe them for beating us back in—"

He jumped and shrieked when Nugget whacked his butt with a reverberating metallic clang. "Let everyone have their moment, fart-face," Nugget said.

"I'll fart in your face," Pickaxe muttered, holding his hands protectively over his rear end.

"I have no doubt that you will," Nitro said. She threw one arm around each brother, grinning as she pulled them in tight. "We're going to win a lot of titles for you, Strike. The Miners' dynasty starts today." She huddled everyone up, putting out a gloved fist.

Everyone slapped their hands on top of hers.

"Miners together!" she bellowed.

"Miners forever!" everyone yelled back. Behind Nitro's

lead, they charged through the tunnel toward the playing field, their war cries amplifying into a deafening wall of sound.

Strike started to run out behind them, but he paused, slowing to a halt. Standing back, he shoved his hands into his jumpsuit pockets, watching in silence as his players burst out into the arena in formation. They thundered toward their opponents, roaring at the tops of their lungs, primed and ready for the smashmouth battle to come.

Drawing in a deep breath, Strike held it for a long moment before exhaling.

With a bittersweet smile on his face, he made his way down the empty tunnel and headed out toward his coach's box.

ACKNOWLEDGMENTS

I can't say enough about our team. Ben Rosenthal is The Editor—that's capital T, capital E—authors can only dream about. The entire squad at HarperCollins is amazing, from contracts to copyediting to cover design to commercial sales. And Alec Shane continues to be The Man, my agent extraordinaire.

I'm so grateful for all the support and help I've gotten from so many friends and family members. At the very top of the list is one standout who's always by my side, no matter what. There aren't enough capital letters to describe how important and incredible she is, so I'll simply say that, year after year, now and for always, JILL DENNY is my lifelong MVP.